the Upside
of Falling

the Upside of Falling

ALEX LIGHT

HARPER TEEN
An Imprint of HarperCollinsPublishers

HarperTeen is an imprint of HarperCollins Publishers.

The Upside of Falling
Copyright © 2020 by Alex Light
All rights reserved. Printed in the United States of America.
No part of this book may be used or reproduced in any manner whatsoever without
written permission except in the case of brief quotations embodied in critical articles
and reviews. For information address HarperCollins Children's Books,
a division of HarperCollins Publishers, 195 Broadway, New York, NY 10007.
www.epicreads.com

wattpad

Library of Congress Control Number: 2019946006

ISBN 978-0-06-291806-2

Typography by Corina Lupp
22 23 24 25 26 LSB 13 12 11 10 9
❖
First paperback edition, 2021
Originally published by Wattpad in 2017.

To my ten-year-old self,
whose dream was to publish a book.

Becca

THERE WERE CERTAIN DAYS I could remember like they were yesterday. The summer morning when my mom finally learned how to bake, which, coincidentally, was also the day our apartment stopped smelling like a smokehouse. Or when I was ten and learned how to ride my bike without training wheels. But remembering wasn't always a good thing. There were days I would give anything to forget. Like the day my dad left. Or the first time I flunked a math test.

Then there were the days that made up most of my life, the ones that were completely unnoteworthy, blending into one another. I had gotten into the habit of ending every day with the same question: Was it worth remembering or forgetting?

Today was on a one-way ticket to being forgotten. And first period hadn't even begun yet.

I was sitting with my back against the last standing oak tree at Eastwood High, a book resting on my knees. It was my favorite reading spot on campus. Tucked away behind the football field, it was far enough away for privacy, but not totally isolated. I could still see morning practice and the members of the football team who were running around with their shirts off. That was enough to indicate that fall was nowhere to be found here in sunny Georgia. Although I'm certain they'd still be shirtless even if the weather dropped below zero. Apparently showing off one's abs trumped potential frostbite.

Peering up from my book, I quickly snuck a glance at the team. It was nothing more than a little peek, but it was enough to notice the groups of students that were lined up on the sides of the field. They were mostly girls. I had to give it to them. Getting out of bed early just to watch football practice? It took dedication. Plus, it wasn't any stranger than getting up early to read in peace.

I'd thought my love for romance novels would have died with my parents' divorce. Instead, it made me crave them more. I was going through two books a week. I could not get enough. It was like, if love couldn't exist in reality, at least it was alive in fiction. Between the pages it was safe.

The heartbreak was contained. There was no aftermath, no shock waves. I mean, there's a reason all books end right after the couple gets together. No one wants to keep reading long enough to see the happily ever after turn into an unhappily ever after. Right?

I jumped when the bell rang. The book fell off my leg and I picked it up quickly before the grass stained the pages green. I shoved my things into my school bag before trudging down the hill, across the field, and into the blue-lockered halls that were now alive with students rushing to make it to first period on time. It was kind of fun to watch. The freshmen ran like their lives literally depended on it. Meanwhile the seniors rested lazily against lockers, like the laws of time didn't apply to them. I pushed past all of them, winding my way to English class. I didn't like to be late. Not because I was a Goody Two-shoes or anything. I just despised the way people stared, like arriving after the bell rings makes it open season for dirty looks or something.

"Morning, Miss Copper," I called when I got to class, throwing my teacher a friendly wave. She grunted, turning her eyes back to her computer screen. I smiled to myself. Some things never changed. I could always count on her early morning hostility.

When I was at my desk in the back row, I returned to my book. The characters were kissing now. Could love really make the world stop? Why did it make every female character feel alive? Wasn't she alive *before* she met him? Or was she in some zombie-like, comatose state? How did love change that, and more importantly, why couldn't I seem to get enough of this unrealistic crap?

My thoughts were interrupted when the two girls in front of me caught my attention. One was pointing to the door, the other was straightening the collar of her shirt while fluffing out her hair. That could only mean one thing . . .

Brett Wells walked into class the same way the sun pours in through a window, slow and captivating. Time seemed to stop as he smiled at the teacher and made his way to the desk in front of mine. I glanced at the clock to make sure it hadn't. Just in case.

I had to give it to the guy. I think he may be the one person who could blur the lines between reality and fiction. With that head of hair that was a little more gold than brown, effortless smile, and altogether unwavering perfection, it was easy to lose yourself in his bright blue eyes. He could have walked out of the pages of a book and materialized in front of me. It was no wonder half the student body was in love with him. Even the teachers weren't immune. I think Miss Copper was blushing. Yuck.

Adding to his mystique was the fact that his parents were considered some of the most generous in our entire school.

Before junior year ended, rumors started circulating that his family was going to donate thousands of dollars to redo the football field. They were really well off. Why? I didn't have a clue. But when the school term started a few weeks ago, the goalposts were sparkling, the paint on the field was still fresh, and the bleachers were no longer covered in rust and multicolored gum. The Wellses came through.

Now I was eyeing the navy-blue varsity jacket hanging off the back of his chair. It was like a flag, announcing who he was: Brett Wells, captain of the football team. Not that I knew anything about him other than the whispers I heard or the checks his parents liked to write. But part of me wondered if he was as nice as everyone said. Or if his relationship history really was nonexistent. I mean, with a face like *that*? Doubtful.

"Becca Hart?" Miss Copper asked, pulling me out of my thoughts. "Care to answer my question once you're done with your daydream?"

I felt my neck warm first, then my cheeks. A second later it reached my toes. "What was the question?" I managed to choke out.

"I asked you to define the concept of star-crossed lovers."

I flipped through the pages of my notebook to yesterday's lesson. "Star-crossed lovers are two people whose love is doomed," I read aloud. "There are so many forces working against them that not even the stars can keep them together."

Satisfied, Miss Copper wrote my answer on the blackboard, the scratchy noise of chalk filling the silence that settled over the classroom. When she finally turned back around, my heart rate had returned to normal. Until she said, "And do you think it was worth it? For Romeo and Juliet to fight for each other knowing their love was doomed?"

I usually preferred not to speak out in class. But when the topic was about love in literature, I had a bad habit of going off on cynical mini rants.

I shook my head. "No, it wasn't worth it. Falling in love destroyed both of their lives. What is the point of loving someone when you're certain you can't be together?" I tapped my pencil against my desk, ignoring the students who turned to stare at me. I knew the expressions on their faces all too well. I was used to it by now. They were the same raised eyebrows my mom and best friend gave me. Only I didn't want their pity or reassurance because my mind was made up. No room for negotiation here! Love was destructive, dangerous. It was safer on pages, and these books were enough of an experience for me. I mean, look at Romeo and Juliet. Was the play tragic? Sure. But did I have to worry about a century-long feud coming between me and the nonexistent man I loved? Definitely not.

When Brett turned to glance at me over his shoulder, those thick eyebrows drawn together, I looked down at my notebook. Numbers filled the back cover, scrawled down in yellow highlighter, blue pen, pencil—whatever I had on hand. It was a countdown until graduation, when I could leave this school and its thousands of unfamiliar faces behind.

One more year, I told myself as another hand shot into the air.

"I disagree with that," Jenny McHenry said. The color of her cheerleading uniform matched Brett's varsity jacket. "Love's still worth the risk, even if it can lead to heartbreak." Students were nodding. Miss Copper was too.

"It wasn't just heartbreak," I added. "Romeo and Juliet died."

"They died for each other," another student chimed in.

"And if they didn't, the book still would have ended before showing them grow apart. Love is temporary. It's not some magical cure. That's what Shakespeare was trying to show. That's why they died, because they were naïve enough to think their love could end a war."

"It's easy for you to say that," Jenny said.

The class fell silent.

"What does that mean?" I asked.

"Love. It's easy to ridicule it when you've never felt it."

Her words kind of hit me like a punch to the throat.

I knew she probably didn't mean anything by them. But the thing was, Jenny and I used to be best friends back in freshman year, when we were both inexperienced fourteen-year-old girls going through the motions. Until summer flew by, sophomore year started, and Jenny got her braces off, grew a few inches (so did other parts of her body), and had no interest in being friends. All of a sudden she was popular. She joined the cheerleading squad and racked up a trail of heartbreaks.

After that she started acting all self-righteous, giving out love advice and acting completely condescending that I was single. Like we hadn't been in the same boat a few months ago. Like having a boyfriend made her an expert in all things romance. Puh-lease.

It was bearable at first but now, two years later? It was annoying.

Beyond annoying.

Anyway, Jenny didn't know the details of my parents' divorce. She knew my dad wasn't around—that much was easy to figure out after spending time at my house. But I never talked to her about it. And she never asked. So her words weren't some well-planned insult that knew exactly how low to strike. They were a coincidence. A coincidence that still hurt.

I raised my hand again. "You don't have to be in love to understand it."

"I think you do." Jenny glanced over her shoulder, pointing at the book on my desk. "Books are one thing. But real feelings are different. It's not the same."

I covered the book quickly with my notepad.

Miss Copper cleared her throat, said, "That's enough, Jennifer," and passed around a handout, announcing that the rest of the period would be for silent work. She shot me a look when she said "silent" that had me sinking down in my chair.

For the rest of the class, I scribbled down halfhearted answers, all the while replaying what Jenny said in my mind. She was wrong. I knew a lot about love. I knew there were two kinds: 1) real love and 2) fictional love. The real kind was what I thought my parents had, pre-divorce. The fictional kind was what I'd preferred since.

I shook my head, imagining the negative thoughts tumbling out of my ears, and focused on the worksheet. I glanced up once before the period ended and found Brett looking at me. He had this look on his face like he could read my mind. Or worse, my heart. There was something about it that had me breathing a sigh of relief when the bell rang.

Like I said, this day was heading down a one-way street to being forgotten . . .

Until it wasn't.

It happened when I was standing at my locker, grabbing my biology textbook. That was when a shadow loomed over me.

"Two years later and you're still obsessed with these books." Jenny grabbed *If I'm Yours* from my arms. She looked at the cover and snorted. "Why is he shirtless? And why are her boobs bigger than her head?"

I grabbed the book and tucked it back under my arm protectively.

"Don't you find these romance books unrealistic?" she continued.

I pretended to be looking for something in my locker. "It's part of what makes them enjoyable."

"No wonder you were being so pessimistic back in class. If this is what you read, you're setting yourself up for disappointment."

A few boyfriends later and she thought she was a love guru, bestowing her knowledge on inexperienced mortals such as me. How gracious.

I wondered if she'd still be saying this if she knew about the divorce. If she knew I had a reason for being a pessimistic downer. If she knew what it felt like to love someone and have them walk out on you.

"I have to get to class, Jen. Can you save the unwanted therapy session for tomorrow?"

Jenny, not listening, tucked her curls behind her ears and said, "Don't your parents ever ask you about it?"

I froze. It was that word. Parents. The plural. The assumption that there were two of them.

"Ask me about what?"

"Relationships. I remember your mom used to always talk to us about love back in freshman year. Remember? She always had hearts in her eyes, waiting for one of us to have a crush or something. I wish she could see me now. Huh?"

And, oh my *gosh*, it was just so annoying. Like what was wrong with being single? What was wrong with not having someone's hand to hold and whatever else couples do? Why couldn't a seventeen-year-old just be on her own and everyone be okay with that? Without expecting her to fall in love at any given moment?

I don't know what had these next words spilling from my lips so effortlessly. Maybe it was the hurt I still felt over Jenny choosing popularity over me. Maybe it was the years of her snarky comments relating to my lack of relationships. Or maybe it was to protect these books I clung to like a lifeline, the only reminder that some sort of love could exist.

Whichever it was, I found myself saying, "My mom doesn't have to pester me about being in a relationship because I'm in one."

I waited for the ground to begin to shake. For the walls to cave and the ceiling to follow until we were standing in a pile of rubble and LIAR was burned into my forehead. I waited for my former best friend to point out that I was lying. Instead her mouth fell open a little, and I realized how different she looked from the fifteen-year-old girl I used to know.

"Who is it?" she asked, seeming genuinely interested.

My brain scrambled for something to say. A name. A person. *Anything.* My palms were sweating and every fictional character I'd read about seemed to vanish from my thoughts.

Right when I was about to give up, I felt an arm wrap around my waist. Felt fingers loop through mine.

I looked up to find Brett's eyes. He was smiling.

"Hey, you," he said, staring right at me.

I felt like I had just woken up from a nap and missed the past few minutes of my life.

"Hi," I said slowly, staring at his hand in mine. How did that get there?

Brett was giving me this look, like *c'mon, Becca, get with it.*

Jenny was glancing between the two of us, looking as confused as I felt. Her eyes zeroed in on Brett's arm on my waist and she said, "You guys are dating?"

Right when I was about to say no, we were not, because that would be completely ridiculous, Brett said, and quite effortlessly, may I add, "Just for a few months now. Since summer break. Right?" He looked down at me, waiting.

At this point I was yelling at my brain to send those signals to my mouth that made me, you know, *speak.*

I managed a weak nod.

"We wanted to keep it private," Brett continued, smiling like he was auditioning for a role in a Hollywood film.

Jenny stared. My hands shook. And Brett just stood there, looking as calm as water while my insides were a complete tsunami.

"There's no way you two are dating."

The way she said it was so confident, so cruel. And that hurt the most. Because why was that unbelievable? Then all I could remember was how it felt the first day of sophomore year when I saw Jenny in the halls. When I walked to her locker, excited to tell her about summer break, and she looked at me and laughed. "Do I know you?" she had said before turning back to her new friends. Was that what it was? The difference in social groups? Brett couldn't be interested in a girl who sits against trees and reads. No. He had to date someone of equal social status. Right? Someone popular. Someone like Jenny.

Brett shrugged, seeming unfazed by the entire situation, as if this was a part of his regular daily routine. Like if you snuck a glance at his agenda it'd say "pretend to date Becca Hart at ten before heading over to second period." Easy-peasy.

"Is this, like, some act for drama class?" Jenny continued.

"It's not an act," I said, holding his hand tighter because, why not? Which may have backfired a little because Jenny said, "Prove it."

Then Brett stepped in front of me. His back was to Jenny and his hands were on my cheeks. "Kiss me back," he whispered when his face was an inch from mine.

And then it felt like my heart was tumbling down, down, down. All the way until it hit the center of the earth. And, wow, maybe those books were kind of onto something about this whole kissing-making-time-stop thing because with Brett's lips on mine, it kind of felt that way.

Brett

MY FIRST THOUGHT WAS THAT I probably shouldn't have done that.

Becca's arms were still around my neck, and she was staring up at me with these wide, alert eyes. From this close, I could see the freckles on her nose, and her hair looked like a massive blur, pushed behind her ears like tangles of sunshine.

I never go around kissing strangers. I didn't really go around kissing anyone.

I could feel Jenny watching us the entire time but when I turned around, she was gone, halfway down the hallway.

I turned back to Becca. "So," I began. "You okay?"

15

She coughed. Her eyes seemed to land on every spot in the hallway except for my face. "Yeah," she said.

I leaned against the locker, trying to not laugh. "You know, that kiss wasn't half bad."

At that, her eyes finally landed on mine. Her cheeks turned red. The color was swallowing up her freckles. She picked up her bag off the floor, holding a book in the crook of her arm.

"I need to get to third period," she said.

"It's second period."

"That's what I said."

She took off down the hall. If she walked any faster, she'd be sprinting.

Not the best reaction to a first kiss, for the girl to run away from you.

The sun was still high in the sky when school let out. I met Jeff, my closest friend on the team, at my car and we drove back to my house. My parents weren't home. My dad had taken the day off work to go to some event with my mom. They were always going to events, waving checks around and making a name for themselves in our small town. My dad's money was part of the reason our football team was the best in the state. It bought us new gear every few months and kept the field in perfect shape.

My dad was proud of our team. More proud of me. He played football in high school too. Team captain. His talent earned him a full scholarship to Ohio State, but then my mom got pregnant with me during senior year. My dad gave up football to stay home with her and raise me. That's why this team meant so much to him, and to me. I was continuing the dream he never had the chance to live out.

My mom loved all the perks marriage gave her. The social standing. The money. The clothes her friends envied and the celebrity status her last name carried. My parents never thought they'd be so wealthy after getting pregnant at eighteen. But my dad went back to college after I was born and got a degree in finance. Now he's the CFO of United Suites, a hotel chain throughout the country. He travels a lot for work. My mom doesn't like it, but she doesn't complain. The money's enough to keep everyone happy, even when he's gone for weeks. He always comes back for my football games, though. He's never missed one.

Jeff and I were in the backyard, throwing the football back and forth. "There's no off time if you want to be the best" was what my dad always said. It replayed in my head like a mantra every day, reminding me not to let him down. I was repeating it when Jeff threw the football. I jumped for it and missed.

"You've had a girlfriend for a day and it's already ruining

your game!" he called. Looked like the news traveled fast around school.

I picked up the ball and threw it back. A perfect spiral. "Still better than yours!" It slammed into his chest and he fell backward on the grass, laughing. I jogged over and tossed him a water bottle.

"When did that start?" he asked.

"What?"

"Your"—he waved his hand around—"relationship."

"Oh. End of summer." The words came out quickly. I hadn't even decided if I was going to go along with this relationship yet. Girlfriends weren't my thing. Neither was high school drama.

"And you didn't think to tell me or the team?"

I shrugged. "You know how people talk at school. I don't want my relationship being gossiped about."

"Everyone is already talking about you," he pointed out.

"Yeah, for carrying the team to finals," I teased, slapping his shoulder. "Not for who I date."

Truth was, I'd never dated in high school. There were girls, crushes here and there, but it never turned into anything more. I was always so focused on football, keeping my head in the game to make my parents proud, that I never had time for dating. I wasn't into the whole one-night thing like the other guys on the team. I wanted the kind of love my parents had—real love—but I wasn't in any rush to find it.

The gate opened then and my parents walked into the backyard, hand in hand, looking way too dressed up to be standing beside Jeff and me, drenched in sweat. My mom's heels were sinking into the grass with every step.

"Dad!" I grabbed the football and jumped up. "We were just taking a quick break. Wanna join?"

He slapped my shoulder. My mom was smiling, gazing between the two of us.

"Next time," he said.

"Your dad has to pack, Brett. He's leaving tonight for New York," said Mom.

"But the first game of the season is on Friday. You can't miss it." I hated sounding like a whiny five-year-old, but my dad never missed a game.

"My flight lands Friday morning. I'll be there."

I smiled, breathing again, and watched them walk back inside. I never cared for the money or the status. I loved my parents and our family. The rest was a bonus.

Jeff was looking up at me oddly.

"What?" I asked.

He shook his head. "Nothing. I should go. My mom needs me home to babysit before she leaves for the night shift."

I nodded, throwing him the keys to my car. "Take it."

"Brett—"

"*Take it*," I insisted. "I'll pick it up tomorrow before school."

He smiled, spinning the keys around his finger. "Thanks, man. I'll see you tomorrow."

I headed back inside. My mom was in the kitchen, cutting up carrots and something green and leafy. She tossed it all in the blender, poured it into a cup, and slid it across the counter.

"Thanks." I drank all of it, trying not to breathe in the smell. "You look different."

She fluffed out her hair. "I dyed it a shade darker this morning. Your father thought it would look nice."

I nodded, unquestioning.

"We're leaving for the airport in an hour if you want to come."

I did . . . but I needed some time to think over what happened today in the hall. I shook my head. "Tell me when you're leaving so I can say bye to Dad."

My mom nodded, then walked around the counter and wrapped me in her arms. She was tiny, barely five feet tall. My dad always said her personality was bigger than her. I never really understood that, though. She wasn't very talkative, unless they were around other people. My mom was quiet. Even her smiles seemed to hide secrets.

"Everything okay, Mom?"

"Everything is great. Go study."

I headed upstairs, grabbed my laptop, and searched for Becca's online profile. It came up instantly and I sent her a friend request. She had under one hundred friends. Okaaaay. All her interests were book-related—bookstores, authors, fan accounts. Her display picture was her and a girl with brown hair smiling together in a kitchen. They were baking, with flour and frosting on their faces. I kept scrolling. *Senior at Eastwood High School, Crestmont, Georgia, USA.* I scrolled some more; there were hardly any posts. There! Four months ago, someone asked for her cell number for a group project. I typed it into my phone and hit save. I told myself it wasn't really creepy, since we'd already kissed. Right?

I was staring at my phone, contemplating calling her, when my bedroom door opened and my dad walked in. "We're about to leave," he said, walking to the edge of my bed. "Are you talking to a girl?"

I put my phone down. "No. No girl."

"You know," he said, sitting down, "your mother and I met when we were your age. Everyone told us we wouldn't beat the odds, getting married so young, but look at us.

21

We're here. We've got you, a great life, and enough money to give you a good future."

I smiled. "I know, Dad." He always went off like this, talking about the past. If there was one thing my parents were proud of aside from me, it was their money. Their well-earned lifestyle, as they liked to call it.

"Playing college ball is going to be your priority once you graduate, Brett. Right now, in high school? This is your prime. You need to get out there. I love your mom, but I think we both have regrets about high school and what we missed out on."

I was confused and a little uncomfortable. "What are you saying?"

"I'm saying, you'll have the time to settle down when you're older. You should be dating now, playing ball. You've never brought a girl home. . . ." My father's voice trailed off, waiting for me to correct him. He was right. I never had.

"Are you dating anyone right now?" he continued. "Any girl you're interested in?"

The problem with having a dad you idolized was that you never wanted to let him down. Every test I aced, touchdown I scored—my dad bragged about all of them. My accomplishments were his accomplishments. What he couldn't do in high school was what he expected me to do in high school. So when he asked if there was a girl, saying yes technically wouldn't be a lie. . . .

I grabbed my phone and pulled up Becca's profile again.

"Her name's Becca," I said, showing him the screen. He took his glasses off and squinted his eyes against the light.

He slapped my shoulder. "When do we get to meet her?"

"When you get back from your trip," I said.

My dad said he was proud of me before he left, rolling his suitcase behind him. I fell back on my bed and groaned. Within a five-minute conversation I'd manage to dig this shallow, fake-girlfriend-sized hole into a full-out grave. There was only one thing to do now: fully commit.

I grabbed my phone and texted Becca's number. *Hey, it's your boyfriend*, I typed. *Need a ride to school tomorrow? For fake-dating purposes*, I added last minute. Then a plain smiley face. No wink. Too creepy.

She responded instantly.

Brett? she wrote back.

How many fake boyfriends do you have? I typed back, laughing.

Very funny.

I asked about the ride again, then for her address. She agreed, writing back the address for an apartment building and to meet her on the street. I told her I'd see her tomorrow, and that we'd work out the details of . . . whatever this was.

An hour later, my mom was back from the airport.

She stopped by my room to say good night, then headed to bed. I heard the sound of the television playing and the water running. Weird. I listened closer, called her name a few times. She didn't answer. When the water stopped some time later, I went to check on her. She was lying in bed sleeping, dozens of tissues bunched up on the empty side of the bed. My dad's side. She cried sometimes when he left. I figured it was because she missed him while he was gone. The next morning, she was always better.

I grabbed a garbage can from the bathroom, cleaned up the tissues, turned off the TV, then headed back to bed. I needed to get some sleep. Something told me tomorrow would be crazy.

Becca

I STAYED UP LATE WRITING in my notebook. It was 1:00 a.m.; my eyes were strained and I couldn't stop yawning. My mom had fallen asleep hours ago. I could hear her snoring through the wall. The reason for my sudden lack of sleep was a full-page pro-con list for continuing on with this fake relationship. "When in doubt, list it out" was my go-to motto. At least in my head.

PROS: Brett's cute (obvious? Yes. Superficial? Very), Mom will finally lay off about me being single, Jenny's snarky comments cease (sounds better than saying it's a revenge scheme), will gain secondhand popularity! (just kidding), maybe finally attend a football game?

CONS: Brett's cute, like, too cute (what do I say to him?

What do we have in common?), Mom will also be waaaaay too invested in this relationship (note: keep this a secret from Mom), Jenny is scary, popularity means being social, I know nothing about football.

Clearly, I was tied between the two.

When the clock showed it was nearly two, I decided to sleep on it. I'd see how I was feeling the next morning, talk it over with Brett, and we could decide together. I mean, he was as much a part of this as I was. I already had no idea why he kissed me today; I ran away too quickly to ask. What did he plan on getting out of this relationship anyway?

I wished I could shut my brain off.

I shut my eyes instead. This could be tomorrow's problem.

The next morning my stomach was in knots. And those knots were tied into another set of knots. Now that my frenzied excitement from that kiss had faded, I was stuck staring straight into reality: that I had gotten myself into a fake relationship with Brett Wells. No pro-con list could save me now.

I texted my best friend, Cassie, an SOS, then got ready for school. One look in the mirror told me staying up late had not been a good idea (hello, eye bags), and my hair was sticking up in every direction, like a flock of birds had built a nest in there while I slept. Overall, not a good start to my day.

The morning got slightly better when I walked into a kitchen covered in cupcakes. The counter, the table, and even the stovetop—all cupcakes. The frosting dripped off the edges, leaving sugary globs everywhere. There was a pink note with my name scrawled on it in the middle of the table. I plucked it up and licked the frosting off my finger. *A cupcake for my cupcake. Have a great day at school. Love, Mom.* I smiled at the note my mom left. It was how every morning started since my father left. There had been hundreds of these notes now.

At first, my mother's baking was horrible. Like, inedible levels of horror. She made frosting from salt instead of sugar. Her pancakes could dent a wall if you threw one hard enough. But she didn't stop. I think baking was her therapy. It was all she did after he left. Like she had to be strong for me, so she bottled up all the pain, and the only way she could release it was by mixing flour and eggs into a bowl and whisking all her sadness away. That first summer, she'd drive us to the bookstore and fill her bag with books about cakes, cookies, cupcakes, and everything sweet. Once she got home, she'd flip to a page at random and spend the rest of the night baking.

Eventually her skills improved. She became good enough to open her own bakery in town. Her friend and business partner, Cara, handled the business and my mom handled the baking. Her sadness was baked into cupcakes and served in pink-and-silver wrappers.

The front door slammed open and Cassie whipped into the kitchen like a hurricane, wearing her pastel-pink Hart's Cupcakes uniform polo. Surprisingly, Cara agreed to use our last name for the business. The first person employed was Cassie, her daughter. I helped out during the summer when school was out. Being a year older and having already graduated, Cassie was working full-time. She was in it more for the free dessert than the money.

"Cupcakes this morning!" she yelled, grabbing one in each hand and taking a bite. "Can you believe it's been two years and I'm not sick of these yet?

"So," she said, licking frosting off her finger, "you sent an SOS. What happened?"

I explained the whole Brett situation. I told her about English class, Jenny, the kiss, and my hasty getaway. By the time I finished, Cassie was speechless.

In two years of being friends, I'd never seen her speechless.

"Wow," she finally said. "You need to tell your mom. She's going to *freak*."

"My mom doesn't need to know her daughter's first boyfriend is fake," I said. It was a bit embarrassing.

"Then leave out the whole fake part. It'll be nice to have someone, don't you think? Like, to be with at school? You've been a hermit ever since I graduated last year."

"Not a hermit," I added.

"A hermit," she repeated. "The only person you hang out with is me and those books."

"Then doesn't that make you a hermit too?"

Cassie shrugged, unwrapping her second cupcake. "You may have a point. You're a hermit by choice, though. It's different. You choose to isolate yourself from other people. I, on the other hand, don't *choose* to. People, for some reason, don't like me."

"Maybe it's because you barge into their apartment and eat all their food."

When she smiled, there was chocolate stuck between her front teeth. "Definitely not that." Cassie stood up, washed her hands, then followed me into the hallway.

"Maybe it was the speech you gave at graduation?" I asked, watching the smile stretch across her face.

"You mean when I told my entire class I hated them?"

"That's the one."

"My dad always said to go out with a bang." We both laughed. It was too ridiculous not to. Our moms always said

29

we were an odd pairing. I tried hard to go unnoticed while Cassie went out of her way to stand out. But when we met two years ago when the bakery opened, we clicked.

"Today's going to be weird. Read any books on fake dating?" she asked.

I shook my head. "I wish."

My phone buzzed. Cassie squealed. Goodbye, three years of living life under the high school radar. I had mastered the art in sophomore year: eat lunch alone, always have headphones or a book on hand, don't make eye contact longer than one second, place your bag on empty chairs to avoid people sitting beside you—the list went on. I was a pro. And all that ended today.

Now there were butterflies living *on* the knots in my stomach.

"Is it him?" Cassie yelled, staring at my phone.

It was. The message said: *Here.*

The butterflies multiplied.

"He's here," I repeated. Cassie's hands were on my back, pushing me out the door and into the hall.

"Have fun," she said. "Text me hourly updates and the names of any student that gives you a hard time."

"Why? So you can fight them with your noodle arms?"

"Violence is not my weapon of choice, dear Becca. Cupcakes are." I raised an eyebrow. "Sometimes students stop by Hart's Cupcakes after class. I'll admit, it's another reason I don't enjoy working there, but now it'll prove useful. So send me some names and I'll spit in their frosting."

"You're disgusting."

Cassie blew me a kiss, yelled, "Have fun with your boyfriend!" then shut the door to my apartment in my own face. I made a mental note to tell my mom to change the locks—or ask her why Cassie even had a key—and stepped into the elevator. My heart lurched into my throat. Not so much from the elevator ride, but rather because of the boy waiting for me downstairs, whose hand I'd have to hold and face I'd have to kiss to sell some lie I never should have even told.

God. What had I done? And what was Brett possibly getting out of this arrangement? It wasn't like his popularity status needed a boost. Come to think of it, it would probably take a steep hit.

By the time I was standing outside, I was sweating. Partly from the sun, which, of course, was placed strategically behind Brett's car, making him glow. And of course he drove a freaking convertible. And of course he was leaning against it with his arms crossed, like some magazine ad come to life. Why couldn't he drive something normal? Less cool? Like a minivan? The ones with the trunk that opens when you kick it?

Our eyes met and he grinned. "Morning, girlfriend," he said. When he leaned in to kiss my cheek, I mentally reminded my brain to tell my heart to continue beating.

"I brought you something," I said, reaching into my bag.

His grin grew until it took up his entire face. "You did?"

I handed him the cupcake I'd snuck when Cassie wasn't looking. "My mom baked it," I explained.

His gaze traveled from the cupcake to my eyes, then back again. He was looking at me like I'd just handed him a million dollars instead of a half-squished cupcake.

"Thanks, Becca." He then proceeded to shove the entire thing into his mouth in that way guys do. "This is really good," he said, crumbs falling onto his shirt.

I got into the car, shrieked when my legs touched the burning hot leather seat, then silently reprimanded myself when Brett started laughing. We were driving through the streets, and I was racking my brain for something to say, when Brett asked, "Your mom bakes a lot?"

I'd thought we'd dive right into the so-what-the-hell-is-going-on-with-us conversation and skip the small talk, but guess not.

"Yeah. Every morning I wake up and my kitchen is covered in cupcakes, pancakes—pretty much any type of cake. She's obsessed."

He nodded. "That's really cool. My mom never bakes. She's more of the wine-and-cheese-tray type."

I wasn't really sure how to respond to that so I just nodded.

We reached a red light. Brett turned in his seat to face me. "As your boyfriend, do I get a cupcake every morning?" I must've looked surprised, because he said, "What?"

"I wasn't sure if you wanted to . . . continue this."

The light turned green.

"Do you?" he asked.

"I'm not completely against it."

Brett laughed. It was contagious. It felt good to laugh with him, like some of the awkwardness had lifted.

"First you run away when I kiss you. Now you want to break up with me when we haven't even been dating for a day. Way to break a guy's heart, Hart." He poked my leg. "See what I did there?"

I was beginning to understand why so many people wanted to be around him. Maybe the rumors were true: Brett really was just a nice guy. Was that why he'd helped me yesterday?

"So you want to go through with this?" I asked. "Pretend to be dating? Fool everyone at school?"

"If I get more cupcakes out of it, sure." He winked at me. His eyes were clear in the sunlight. I wanted to ask what else he was getting out of this relationship. I mean, my mom's cupcakes were good. But they weren't *that* good to warrant this entire mess. But then we pulled into the school parking lot, and the butterflies in my stomach I momentarily forgot about were back. Trillions now.

I gulped. Opened the window. Closed the window. *Breathe, lungs. Breathe.*

"Um," I said, completely stalling. "We should, like, figure out the rules to all of this."

"Can we do that later? I don't think you want to be late to first period."

I glanced at the time. Class started in five minutes and I still had to stop at my locker. Just picturing Miss Copper's glare had me hopping out of the car at full speed. Brett ran around to my side, grabbed my shoulder. I think he could see how panicked I felt.

"It'll be okay," he said.

"Miss Copper scares me," I said. "I don't want to be late."

"Right. That's why you're freaking out."

I sighed. From the way Brett was standing and how close he was, the parking lot was entirely blocked from my view. If people were staring, I couldn't see them. But I knew they could see me. See *us*. What would they say? What would they think? Would they even believe that Brett Wells would date me? I was completely overwhelmed. It took every ounce of determination to throw my backpack over my shoulders and take a step toward the door.

"I know you might be used to all this attention, Brett. But I'm not. This is new for me, and it's terrifying. I just . . . need a minute."

"That's cool. We can wait. Miss C doesn't scare me," he added.

I breathed through my nose, then through my mouth. I counted to ten, closed my eyes, and focused on my feet planted on the ground. When I opened them, Brett was watching me. He didn't look annoyed, though. He was just standing there, waiting, that hopeful look on his face.

"Ready?" he asked, holding out his hand.

"No," I said, taking it anyway.

Then he was tugging me to the front door.

"I don't really like the attention either," he said while we walked, probably trying to distract me from the students. I stared directly in front of me, not letting my eyes wander. "That was the one reason I wasn't sure I wanted to go through with this. I don't like people talking about my dating life. It's none of their business."

"Yeah," I said, half paying attention. "That makes sense."

He was chuckling, literally dragging me through the hall.

The first person I saw was Jenny, standing beside the

office with her cheerleading squad. I quickly looked away, following the first rule in how-to-live-life-under-the-radar. Brett was oblivious, towing me behind him as he moved through the halls. A personal human shield. It took me a minute to stop staring at my feet and realize we were standing in front of my locker. I grabbed my books in record speed and made a dash for English class. At this point, Brett probably thought I was insane, which, for the record, may be partially true.

Class wasn't as bad as I expected. We made it in time, so no glaring today. Brett tried to sit at the empty desk beside mine, but it turns out not even his charms were exempt from the horror of assigned seating. Brett lasted a whole two minutes before Miss Copper yelled for him to return to his seat. The class laughed, and it felt a little easier to breathe after that. Aside from Jenny turning to stare at me every once in a while, there were no disturbances. No one commented on yesterday's conversation. No one grilled me about Brett. It was just another day in English class.

Talk about anticlimactic.

The first half of the day was smooth sailing, until lunch came around. I used to sit in the cafeteria with Jenny, just the two of us. We'd each buy something different to eat and share it. For sophomore and junior year, I ate with Cassie. After she graduated, I started eating outside alone. There were a few dozen picnic tables scattered across the yard. You had to get there pretty early to grab a good spot, which was why I opted to bring a lunch instead of waiting in the cafeteria line. There was one table hidden under a tree that was my favorite. I was planning on eating there today until Brett texted, saying he saved me a spot inside.

I mean, my expectations weren't even *that* high. I figured he saved the two of us a table, probably in the corner so we could talk this all over without someone hearing. Instead, I walked into the cafeteria to find him sitting smack in the center. It was the jock table, lined with every member of the football team. The cheerleading squad sat at the next table over. Jenny et al.

I lasted all of one second before dashing toward the exit doors. I mean, come on! Did Brett really expect me to sit with his teammates, listen to them debate football game plays and talk about how we supposedly started dating in the summer? Maintaining the facade of our relationship was not worth that level of torture.

I took a seat at my usual table, pulled out my sandwich and book, and started to read. I wasn't even through the first page when Brett texted.

Where are you? it read.

Outside, I typed back.

. . . Why?

I shut my phone off and returned to my book.

A minute later, a shadow loomed over me.

"You stood me up," Brett said, stealing one of my grapes.

"I don't like eating inside." I placed the bookmark on the page and looked up. "And I really don't want to eat at the jock table, Brett."

"Oh." His eyebrows drew together. "I didn't even think of that. Give me a second."

Before I could ask why, he was running away, back through the cafeteria doors. A moment later he burst through them, holding a tray of food in one hand and his backpack in the other, this huge smile on his face.

"I'm not letting you eat out here alone," he said, taking a seat. "We have an image to uphold, sweetie."

I wrinkled my nose. "Sweetie?"

"No? You don't like it? What about babe? Baby?"

I laughed, swatting his hand away when he reached for another grape. "First rule is nicknames are not allowed."

Brett nodded. "Becca it is. What are the other rules?"

"No PDA," I said.

He pouted. "Was the kiss really that bad?"

"I don't like the staring."

"We'll come back to that," he said. "You need to come to my football games every Friday."

"Every Friday? What about every other Friday?"

"Every Friday," he repeated. "Nonnegotiable. And I want you in the stands screaming my name. Remind me to give you my spare jersey."

"Then I'm not eating lunch inside the cafeteria."

"Oh, I already knew that much," he said, taking a bite of his hamburger. "I agree to relocate to this table. What about some kissing? Hand holding? No one's gonna believe we're dating if there's three feet of space between us at all times."

I tried to play it cool. My face was saying, "Yeah, I kiss boys for fun all the time. Done it *loads*. Experienced kisser? That's me, nice to meet you," while my insides were that black-and-white static sound televisions make when the channel doesn't work.

"Fine. Lessen the space and minimal touching. Got it."

Brett grinned. "The best part."

I rolled my eyes.

"We need to have the same story about how this started," I said.

"We probably should have discussed this yesterday."

"I was too busy running away from you," I half joked.

Brett laughed. "Back to this story; what are you thinking?"

It took a second for my brain to sift through every romance book I've read and piece together a situation that could work. "We met at the beginning of summer break,"

I said. "I was in the park reading and you were playing football."

"And I was obviously shirtless," he added.

"Obviously."

"Then you fell madly in love with me—" he said, ducking when I threw a grape at his head. Then I froze because I had just *thrown a grape at Brett's head*. But he was grinning, so I don't think he felt weird about it. "Nice throw. So, one glance at you with your nose buried in a book and my heart was a goner? And we kept our relationship a secret because you didn't want all the attention once school started?"

I nodded, absent-mindedly toying with the pages of my book. "Then I guess that's how our love story began," I said.

"Now we just need to see how it ends."

I only then noticed how long Brett's eyelashes were. They grazed his cheeks every time he blinked, long enough to cause a windstorm of their own. Blink. Blink. Blink. They kept batting as we stared at each other. He had this goofy cartoon smile on his face.

The sun disappeared after that, hiding behind a cloud. He looked different out of the sunlight. It felt like the perfect time to ask the question that had been weighing on me all day. "Why are you doing this?" I finally asked. "You know most girls and plenty of guys in this school would date you.

Like, *real* dating. So why me? Why fake it?"

"I could ask you the same thing," he said, resting his elbows on the table and planting his chin on top, "but I think your answer has something to do with what you said in English class yesterday, about how dangerous love is."

I shrugged. "My parents had a weird divorce. What's your excuse?"

"The opposite. My parents have this perfect marriage—"

"So it seems."

"See? Everyone knows about it. It's like some citywide Cinderella story or something. My dad always gives me these talks on how I should date in high school, play the field like he never could."

"Why couldn't he?"

"My mom got pregnant with me when she was a senior. My dad gave up football, his scholarship—everything for her. For me. It's like he wants me to continue living from where he left off. You know?"

I nodded, thinking about my mom's persistence that I date and find the love she lost. "Yeah," I said. "I really do."

"But I'm not interested in dating in high school," Brett continued. "I've got good grades and a good thing going with football. I have my parents and that's enough for me. I always wanted to leave settling down for after college. But my dad doesn't see it like that."

"So a fake girlfriend is just what you need. Keeps your dad happy and takes the pressure off you."

"Kind of makes me sound like a dick," he said.

"I don't think so," I said. "In a way, it's like we're mutually using each other. And we can just be friends along the way."

Brett pointed at my sandwich. "You gonna finish that?" I pushed the tray across the table to him. "Thanks. So what's up with you and Jenny? That argument was intense."

I explained the odd, unspoken tension we'd had since freshman year. Then Brett said, "That kiss must've really pissed her off."

"I think so."

Brett finished the sandwich, brushed his hands on his T-shirt, then reached across the table. "So we'll pretend to be dating for a few months, then have a mutual breakup, and part as friends. Deal?" he asked.

For once, I tried not to overthink this. I shook his hand. "Deal."

Brett grinned. "Great," he said, then pointed back to the book between us. "So, if this were one of your books, who would we be?"

"That depends," I said. "What kind of book is it? A

romance? Mystery? Fairy tale?"

"Fairy tale," Brett said very seriously.

"I'm guessing you want to be the prince?"

"Only if you're the princess."

I left school that day with a smile on my face. I wasn't the best actress—I nearly failed sophomore drama class—but, together, we could pull this off. Brett seemed to be nailing the fake-boyfriend role already. I was starting to think he's one of those people who's naturally good at everything.

After last period, Brett met me at my locker and offered to drive me home. I refused, saying I wanted to walk. My mind was nearly reaching overdrive, and I needed a few minutes to be alone and think the day over. This was only day one and I was overwhelmed. Why couldn't I just stick to reading romance books? Why did my life have to become one? Luckily, like my romance novels, this was all fake. And there was no danger in that.

It was kind of like getting the best of both worlds: a relationship without the risk of heartbreak.

Lost in thought, I didn't even think about where my feet were taking me until I was passing the park that connected to the street my father lived on. Part of me was ashamed to know the directions to his house by heart. I saw the address once on a letter that came in the mail addressed to my mom. I think it was a check he sent for child support. I scribbled the address down, then pretended I never saw it.

I was thirteen the first time I walked here. The house was empty. There were no cars in the driveway. I felt so guilty that I didn't return for another year. It was like a betrayal to my mom to be here, chasing after him when *he* left *us*. The next time, he was sitting on his porch. I had to hide behind a tree so my dad wouldn't see me.

I started visiting once a month after that. Eventually there was another woman. She'd open the door when his car pulled into the driveway and kiss him hello. She had long, curly black hair. Nothing like my mom's short blonde bob. I never told her he was dating someone. I wasn't sure if she wanted to know. Or if she even cared anymore.

Now I was standing at the end of the street, six houses down, behind a bush that came halfway up my knees. His house was on the corner, with a wraparound porch and a two-car garage that was painted the color of the sky.

I never got close enough that my father could look out a window and spot me. I didn't want to risk him seeing me. Ever. I wasn't entirely sure my dad would even recognize me now. I had changed a lot in five years. At least on the outside.

It still hurt to think about how he left. How he never

looked back. My mom got full custody of me too. They never even went to court. He just agreed. They signed the papers and then it was done. I didn't really understand it when I was twelve. I thought I'd spend weekends with my dad and weekdays with my mom like I'd seen in movies. But then months passed by and he never picked me up. Whenever I asked my mom, she said he was busy. I later learned my dad wanted what was considered a "fresh start." And you couldn't have that with a twelve-year-old, a walking reminder of your past.

The hardest part was that it was so unexpected. My parents never fought. There weren't any signs. Then again, I was a kid and probably would have missed them anyway. But there was nothing that stood out in my mind. I remembered my mom leaving for work in the morning—back when she was a nurse—and my dad kissing her goodbye. He was home during the day and worked night shifts at a warehouse in town. He picked me up from school. He bought me ice cream in the summer and hot chocolate in the winter. There were no bad memories. No moment that I can pinpoint and say *yeah, that's where everything went wrong*. I never bothered to ask my mom either. We never talked about it. I was too scared to hurt her. So we dodged the subject by baking and reading and I was left always wondering why he left. Maybe that's why I still came here, for answers.

I waited twenty minutes (it was always twenty minutes) for his car to pull into the driveway. He stepped out wearing a gray suit, glasses low on his nose, and was barely up the driveway before the front door was pulled open and the woman walked out. I still didn't know her name. I wondered if he knew her before the divorce, or if they met after. Maybe she was the reason he left in the first place.

My dad smiled as he kissed her, then both their hands went to her pregnant belly that had grown a little since I was last here. I watched as he got onto his knees and kissed her stomach. I wondered if a day would come when he'd abandon that child too. I really hoped it didn't. I hoped he'd choose to stick around so that little baby would never have to go through what I did. I hoped they'd never have to hide behind a bush and watch their father love his new family the way he couldn't love his old one.

It was only when the door shut and they went inside that I began to walk home. That night, when my mother asked me where I'd gone after school, I lied.

Brett

EVERY THURSDAY ENDED THE SAME at Eastwood High, with a pep rally after last period. All students filed into the bleachers after the bell rang. The rally would open with the cheerleaders doing a routine and the football team sitting in the front row. There was always some sort of announcement Principal Marcus had to make. Last week, it was that our vice principal was retiring. It would have been sad if the cheerleaders hadn't done a routine directly after.

Today I was running late. Becca agreed we'd go together but she still hadn't shown up at her locker, where we agreed to meet. *Where are you?* I texted, bouncing on the balls of my feet impatiently. *Library*, she sent back, *almost done*. I could hear the band begin to play as I ran down the hall, toward the stairs that led to the library.

I found her sitting in the back corner against a shelf with her legs crossed and a book on her ankles. Lost in whatever she was reading, she didn't notice me standing there until my shoes were touching hers.

"Hey," I said. She jumped and shut the book quickly.

"Hi. Sorry. I was trying to finish this."

I sat beside her and picked up the book in her lap. "*Romeo and Juliet*? You're still reading this?"

"What do you mean *still*?" She grabbed it from my hands and tucked it under her arm. "We have a test on it next week." I nodded, pretending like I knew that. "Did you want to leave?"

"The band just started. We still have a few minutes," I said. "Keep reading."

"Okay."

Becca held that book more carefully than I've seen people hold babies. I couldn't understand why—it was already ripped and frayed at the edges. She read with her finger tracing each line as she went. I had a strange urge to ask her to read out loud, but I was sure that violated the library's number one rule: being quiet.

"I can't read when you're staring at me," she said.

"I'm not staring at you." She looked up quickly and caught me. "I was staring at the book. It looks like it's been through a lot."

"When was the last time you were in here?" she asked.

I thought about it for a second. "Freshman year."

She rolled her eyes. "Wow. *Wow.*"

"Is that the kind of girlfriend you want to be?" I joked. "A judgmental one?"

"You're just . . . such a jock," she said with a laugh.

"I'll have you know I've read all the Harry Potters."

She did not look impressed. At all.

"That doesn't count. Everyone's read Harry Potter. It's practically a childhood rite of passage."

She had a point.

Becca reached for her backpack and our knees bumped against each other's. I stared at her socks sticking out from her sneakers as she packed up her things. They were white, with cat ears on the top. I was laughing when she said, "You know, no one else is in here."

"So?"

"So we don't have to pretend to be dating when no one's around to see us."

Another solid point.

Becca gathered her things and we headed out into the hall. I was leading her toward the door to the field when she tugged on my arm, stopping me. "What?" I asked, a little annoyed. I wanted to be at the pep rally with my team.

"Is it cool if I head home and skip the rally?" She was chewing on her lip like she was afraid to ask me. "I have a calculus test on Monday and I want to start studying."

"Becca, today's Thursday."

She crossed her arms, eyes narrowing. "Exactly. I should've started studying a week ago."

I couldn't decide if she was being sarcastic.

There were hundreds of students in the bleachers already. I doubted anyone would notice if she wasn't there. . . .

"Okay," I agreed. "You're still coming to my game tomorrow?"

"Of course."

I smiled and took a step backward. "Have fun studying, then." Becca waved and headed down the hall, that book still in her hand.

I ran onto the field a few minutes late. The principal was talking and Jeff was waving me down, an empty spot beside him. I snuck in as incognito as possible. "Hey," I whispered.

"You're late," he whispered back.

"Was with Becca." Jeff gave me a look, then turned his attention back to the principal. He probably took that as meaning we were hiding somewhere making out, not sitting in the back of a library. I didn't correct him. At least it added some credibility to this.

The rally ended in an hour, and I was halfway back to my car when my phone rang. It was my mom. I answered on the second ring. "Hey, Mom. What's up?"

"Everything okay?" she asked. "You're usually home by now." I didn't miss the change in her voice. It happened whenever my dad was gone. She sounded kind of lonely. Maybe a little sad.

I reminded her about the pep rally and promised I'd be home soon. I was driving through town when I spotted a bakery and impulsively pulled over. Maybe some desserts would cheer my mom up. A bell rang when I opened the door and the smell of vanilla hit me. There were tables lining the wall and a huge glass dessert display. The place was empty. I walked to the counter and rang the bell. An older woman with short blonde hair came out from the back, smiling.

"What can I get you, hon?"

I wasn't sure what my mom liked since she never really ate dessert, so I got her an assortment. Some cupcakes, some fruit tarts. A few croissants and these white balls with jam in the middle. "Those are my daughter's favorite," the woman said when I pointed at them.

"Then I'll take three," I said. "Do you have any cannoli?" I think I may have seen my mom eat those once at a wedding.

"We're making a fresh batch now. They should be ready." She turned around and called, "Bells, bring me out some cannoli!"

I smiled and handed her a few bills. "Thank you."

The woman, whose name tag read AMY, was dropping the change into my hand when someone walked out of the back. I looked up and froze. It was Becca. She had flour all over her face and was wearing a pink Hart's Cupcakes T-shirt.

"Becca?" I said slowly.

She dropped the entire tray of cannoli on the floor.

The woman, who could only be her mother based on how similar they looked, spun around and shrieked, clamping her hand over her mouth. "Becca!" she yelled. "What happened?"

"I—" Her cheeks were bright red. My hand was still outstretched over the counter, money in my palm.

"Just clean this up. I'll go get more." Then her mom turned to face me and said, "I'm so sorry, hon. Give me a minute."

As soon as she disappeared into the back, Becca ran to the counter. "What are you doing here?" she whisper-yelled, leaning across and pointing her finger at me.

I held my hands up. "I came to buy some stuff for my mom. I didn't know you worked here . . . Bells."

"It's a nickname," she hissed, "and my mom owns this bakery!" She kept glancing frantically behind her shoulder. "Hart's Cupcakes? Becca *Hart*? You didn't piece the two together?"

Oh.

"I thought you were studying for calculus," I pointed out. She ducked behind the counter and began picking up the broken cannoli shells. "Need some help?"

"No," she snapped, then sighed. "Sorry. I was studying, but my mom called me and asked me to come in and help her. There's a big last-minute catering order for tomorrow morning."

At that, her mom came back in, holding another tray of cannoli. She took three and placed them in a box. "On the house, hon. Sorry about that." She looked between us then, like she'd just realized we'd been talking. "Do you two know each other?" she asked, her face lighting up.

I held out my hand. "Yeah, we do. I'm Brett. Her boy—"

Becca jumped up from the floor and screamed, "Friend! He's Brett. My friend, Mom."

Before I even had a chance to be offended, the door to the back opened and a girl with brown hair stepped out— the girl from Becca's profile picture. She took one look at me, then Becca, then her mom. She grinned, leaning against the wall to watch.

The whole situation was weird, and I was happy when Becca's mom handed me the box of pastries and said, "Nice to meet you, Brett. Enjoy, and sorry again."

I walked out of the bakery in a daze. Becca never mentioned she wanted to keep us a secret from her mother. But **that was clear now.** Crystal clear. And her mom owned a bakery? I really knew nothing about the girl I was supposed to be dating. That had to change. No one was going to believe this otherwise. Then I remembered my game tomorrow night and how my parents were going to be there. With Becca.

I crossed my fingers and hoped that would go well.

And that Becca wouldn't back out last minute.

Becca

FOUR HOURS HAD PASSED SINCE the whole Brett bakery fiasco and my mom still hadn't stopped talking about it. Not because she was mad I dropped an entire tray of cannoli, made from her grandmother's secret recipe. I would have preferred that. Instead she'd been talking about Brett, all googly-eyed and weird.

We were closing up the bakery, just the two of us. Cassie had already left after wishing me luck. She was right. I needed it. My mom's brain had entered that obsessive love zone and there was no escaping until she got it out of her system.

"How do you know each other again?" she asked while sweeping the floor.

"English class," I said for the third time.

"He's your age?"

"Yes, Mom."

"Does he have a girlfriend?"

"Mom!" I threw the wet rag at her. "Can you stop? Please?"

"All I'm saying," she continued, not listening, "is that it sounded like he started to say something before you yelled about you two being friends."

She eyed me suspiciously over the broom.

"I don't know. I'm not a mind reader," I mumbled.

She laughed. "Right, Bells."

I'd be lying if I said part of me wasn't considering telling her Brett and I were dating (leaving out the fake part, duh). *Mom will finally lay off about me being single* was one of the reasons I'd listed in the PRO section of my pro-con list. The happiness she'd feel knowing Brett was my (fake) boyfriend would be enough to last her a lifetime. She'd give me one of her squeeze-the-life-out-of-you hugs and it *could* potentially be a nice moment. . . .

"He's very cute," she continued.

And then she said things like that and ruined it. She got into these obsessive moods that weirded me out. I mean, she was practically ready to plan our wedding after selling him some pastries.

"I hadn't noticed." I was lying. My mom knew it. I knew it. Everyone on Earth knew it. I felt like taping a sign to my head that said "Yes I Am Aware Brett Is Cute and No I Do Not Like Him Like That" and calling it a day.

"Becca." Her voice was all serious now, and she was walking toward me. I kept my eyes on the counter. "You know I want you to be happy," she said, placing her hand over mine.

"I know, Mom." And I did know. She told me all the time.

"And that just because your father and I weren't a match, it doesn't mean you won't find yours."

"Yes, Mom."

"And," she continued, lifting my chin and forcing me to look her in the eyes, "I want you to find someone you love. Someone that's deserving of you."

Urgh. It was so difficult for me to understand how my dad could have left my mother in moments like this. She was caring, kind. She was beautiful too. Like, really beautiful. How could someone not love her? My mother was the greatest person in the world.

"You know divorces aren't—"

"Divorces aren't genetic," I finished. "I knooooow."

She smiled, satisfied.

We cleaned in silence for a little. I couldn't stop thinking about my dad. There were a million questions I wanted to ask about him. Normally they were strictly off-limits. From past experiences, my mom would either 1) cry or 2) become very quiet and retreat to her bedroom. But now she was smiling while she swept, and she kept giving me these hopeful glances. So I took a deep breath and said, "Hey, Mom? When was the last time you spoke to Dad?"

I didn't think she heard me. She kept sweeping, never breaking rhythm. I bit my tongue, figuring it was for the best. But then she said, "When the bakery opened."

I immediately stopped cleaning.

"He came by the second or third day," she continued. "He couldn't believe I learned how to bake. You remember how I always messed up our birthday cakes? He was shocked. You should have seen his face." She was smiling to herself now, lost in thought. "He bought some cannoli—you know how much he loved your grandmother's recipe—and then he left. I haven't heard from him since."

I didn't know what to say.

"The store's clean. Let's lock up, Bells."

I took the broom and the rag and placed them in the closet. We grabbed our jackets, then I followed my mom outside and watched as she locked the doors. Then we headed home.

I didn't ask any more questions. She didn't give any more answers.

There were cupcakes in the kitchen the next morning. Meaning my mom wasn't upset about our conversation the night before. I still couldn't shake the feeling that I'd imagined it, her actually talking about my dad. All night I kept hearing the sound of the bell chiming as the bakery door opened and imagining my dad standing there and what it must have felt like for my mom. Did it hurt? Or was it nice to see him? Did he ask about me? What else did they talk about other than pastries? My head was spinning. The worst part was knowing I'd never have the answers. My mom even telling me she saw him was a miracle. A one-time miracle.

I was still obsessing over it by the time I got to school. Which was why I didn't notice the package at the bottom of my locker until it fell out and landed on my shoe. I picked it up quickly and looked around the hallway. No one was watching me. Inside was a navy-blue football jersey with WELLS stitched into the back in gold thread. There was a note that read *Wear this tonight, girlfriend.* I rolled my eyes. It was ridiculous that my first high school football game was all an act. But the jersey was really soft, and it smelled good, kind of like Brett (why did I know what Brett smelled like?), so I'd wear it.

I called Cassie during lunch. Since tonight was the first game of the season, the football team was meeting with the coach during lunch to discuss the game plan. Which meant no Brett and a whole lot of privacy. I told Cassie about the jersey, and asked her to come to the game with me tonight. She said she wanted to, but had a closing shift at the bakery. I offered to ask my mom to find someone to cover it, but no luck. I was going alone. Maybe the jersey would be big enough for me to hide a book in. If I sat at the back of the bleachers, no one would notice. Right?

Turns out I was right. I tried the jersey on when I got home, and the thing nearly reached my knees. It was five sizes too big, and I almost didn't wear it. But then I remembered how I blew Brett off yesterday with the school rally. . . . Wearing it was the least I could do to pull my weight here.

He didn't respond when I texted that I was on my way. He was probably busy getting ready for the game.

When I got to Eastwood High, the bleachers were completely full. I finally found a spot wedged between two people and sank down. I contemplated reading but there was too much noise to concentrate, so I focused on the crowd instead. The cheerleaders were dancing on the field until, finally, the Bears ran out from the side. Everyone stood up and started screaming. I did the same, remembering this was a part of the deal Brett and I made.

Cheering girlfriend in the stands? Check.

Wearing Brett's jersey? Check.

A shoo-in for Fake Girlfriend of the Year? Check.

I watched the game and pretended to understand what was happening. I should have done research beforehand to at least learn the basics of football. I just stood when everyone else did, screamed when they screamed, and clapped when they clapped. I even made sure to yell extra loud when Brett had the ball—which was for most of the game, really.

After about an hour, I was actually enjoying myself. Maybe this football thing wasn't too bad. It was easy to lose myself in the excitement, and I was beginning to understand why so many people spent their Friday nights sitting out here with blue paint on their cheeks and gold ribbons in their hair. It made you feel like you were a part of something bigger than yourself.

When Brett scored the winning touchdown, the crowd erupted like a volcano. I actually had to cover my ears to prevent permanent damage. I could see the smile on his face as his teammates lifted him above their heads, chanting his name and carrying him around like a trophy. It was kind of cool to be dating him, even if it was fake.

I followed as the crowd trickled from the bleachers and over to the locker room doors, waiting for the players. The night was cool, with stars covering the entire sky like a blanket. I tugged Brett's jersey around me a little tighter to get rid of the goose bumps running along my arms. I was bouncing on my heels, rubbing my hands together to stay warm, when the door finally opened and Brett walked out. Our eyes locked and I expected him to be smiling, not looking sad. His eyes were searching the crowd as he walked toward me.

"You were great," I said lamely when he was in front of me.

It was like the words weren't even registering in his brain.

"Have you seen my parents?" he asked, frantically searching the crowd.

He didn't even look at the jersey I was wearing or comment on my cheering.

"No." I began looking around, as if I'd even recognize them.

"My dad said he'd be here tonight. I haven't seen him. Or my mom." He was mumbling to himself at this point, eyes still scanning.

"I'm sure they're here somewhere, Brett. Text them?"

"Right." He nodded and pulled out his phone. A minute later his face fell.

"What is it?"

"She said my dad had to stay in New York longer. He won't be home till Monday." His fist clenched when he said this, and I didn't miss the way he shoved his phone into his pocket like he was mad at it.

I couldn't understand why he was so angry. His dad missed one game. So what? My dad had missed half my life and I wasn't snapping at people because of it.

This didn't seem like a good time to say that, though.

"He'll be at your next one," I offered.

"I guess. Do you need a ride home?" He looked at me then for the first time, his eyes going down to the jersey. "You wore it." Smallest of smiles. "It looks good on you."

I pulled at the hem self-consciously. "Yeah. Thanks."

"For the ride or the compliment?"

"Both?"

Brett grabbed my hand then and led me through the crowd. We were making our way toward the parking lot; I could see his car parked in the corner. He didn't make small talk this time, and I had a feeling he was still upset about his dad. When we arrived at his car and were sitting inside, I tried again.

"About your dad," I began, "he's really never missed a game?"

Brett began to drive, a little faster than normal. "Never."

"What about your mom? Do they come together?"

"Yeah. She said she didn't want to come alone tonight."

"So what would have happened if they came?"

He glanced at me quickly, then back to the road. "What do you mean?"

"Like . . . Would you have introduced me to them as your girlfriend or something?" I asked, trying to keep his mind off his dad's absence.

Brett laughed, reaching over to flick my knee. "Probably, yeah. I already told my dad about you, remember? He would have wanted to meet you."

For the record, he had not told me that.

"You've really never had a girlfriend before?"

"Never."

"That's weird," I whispered so he wouldn't hear.

We drove past two traffic lights before Brett spoke again. "I know what you're trying to do, Becca. It's not working."

I rolled down the window, letting in the air. "And what's that?"

"Trying to make me forget about the bakery yesterday. And how you stood me up during the rally."

I felt my face heat up just thinking about it. "For the second time, I didn't stand you up! I *was* going to study before my mom called. And believe me, the interrogation I went through that night was punishment enough."

"Interrogation?"

"My mom may be your new number one fan."

"Your mom doesn't even know me," he said.

"Isn't that how it works? Everyone knows bits and pieces about you and loves you anyway?" Now Brett gave me this funny look, his eyebrows drawn together. "What? You're an enigma."

"A what?"

"An enigma," I repeated. "Do you even pay attention in English class? It means a puzzle, a mystery. Whatever."

He was smiling when we pulled into my apartment building.

"I'm not a mystery," he said, "people just make assumptions and no one bothers to find out the truth. That's it."

With the moonlight slanting across Brett's face, this entire conversation had taken a sad turn. Uncomfortable and never being very good with talking about deep stuff, I opened the door and began to get out of the car. Brett's hand wrapped around mine, stopping me.

"Your bag," he said, reaching across the car and picking it up. "Why is this so heavy?" When his hand began to reach inside, I shrieked and tried to pull it away. Too late. Brett was holding my book.

I coughed. Pretended to look confused. "Wow. How did that get in there?"

"You brought a book to my football game," he said, all serious and offended.

I looked over my shoulder, pretending someone was calling me. "I did not."

I was telling so many lies lately I could barely keep track.

Brett placed it back in my bag and handed it to me. At this point I was half in and half out of the car. My back was beginning to hurt.

"Was being at the game that bad?" he asked.

This time, I was honest. "Not at all. I kind of liked it."

"So no book next time?" He was giving me puppy eyes.

I caved. "No book next time."

I waved goodbye and was halfway to the doors when Brett called my name. The window was rolled down, his head sticking out of the car like a dog. "What are you doing tomorrow?" he yelled.

I had this irrational fear my mother would hear this conversation from eleven floors up and come barging outside like a shark smelling blood. I shushed him and quickly ran to the car. "Nothing. Study—"

"Studying for calculus. I know. What else?"

I blew out a breath, thinking. "That's it." Pause. "I have a very intense social life."

Brett laughed, and it was like whatever heaviness weighing him down earlier was entirely gone. "Do you want to hang out tomorrow? There's something I want to show you."

I felt my face scrunch up. "Is this, like, a date? For show or something?" I didn't want this relationship to start taking up my weekends too. A five-day school commitment was enough. Plus my Friday nights!

He shook his head. "Not this time. Just two friends, together. You said I was a mystery. Right?" I nodded. "Then let me show you I'm not. It doesn't make much sense if my own girlfriend doesn't know anything about me."

He made a good point.

"I know you like football."

"I like other things too."

"Like what?"

"Come with me tomorrow and find out," he said, grinning.

The guy was good. I'll give him that.

"Pick me up at two," I said. Then I ran inside before my mom could look out the window and spot us together.

Brett

I WAS TEN MINUTES LATE to Becca's apartment. I was still obsessing over my dad and spent almost an hour trying to call him. Where was he? Even my mother said she hadn't heard from him since yesterday. What was he doing that was so important he couldn't text either of us back? I told myself he was busy, probably in another meeting—or maybe he got an early flight to come home tonight. It would justify why he wouldn't call, and it was easier to think of than him simply forgetting.

But my dad didn't forget. So there had to be an explanation for all of this.

I ended up going to the gym in the morning with Jeff just to get my mind off it. He wasn't any help. When I told him about my dad, he blew up, said it wasn't a good idea to idolize people because they can never live up to your expectations. But this wasn't a celebrity or some random person in a magazine. This was my dad, and there had to be a reason why he didn't show up. I only hoped everything was okay.

Either way, I was pretty sure Jeff was pissed at me. Which wasn't unusual. He had a rough time at home, watching his sister while his parents worked around the clock, so sometimes his frustration boiled up and I happened to be in the line of fire. I wasn't mad. He'd apologize on Monday and we'd be cool again, back to talking about football.

Now I was waiting in my car for Becca to come outside, preferably with something for me to eat from her mom's bakery. When she finally walked out a minute later, a brown paper bag in hand, I wasn't disappointed. She was smiling when she opened the door, and I realized that this—the two of us hanging out—could be a new kind of normal.

"Afternoon," she said, waving the bag in front of me. "I brought you a surprise."

I was already feeling better.

"Cupcakes?" I asked, sniffing.

"No. It's better than that." I reached for the bag and she pulled it away, stuffing it into the side of the door before I could reach it. "It's for later," she explained. "If I like what we do today, you can eat it."

"And if you don't like it?"

She smiled. Maybe the biggest one yet. "Then you can watch me eat it."

I started driving through town with purpose then. The good thing about living in Crestmont, a town with under ten thousand people, was that it's so small you could drive through the entire thing in less than ten minutes. We had one high school, one church, one gym, one theater—pretty much one of everything. There were a few run-down hotels and diners lining the interstate for travelers stopping for the night. And it was always one night. People passed through Crestmont like a revolving door. No one wanted to stay. Unless you were born here and had no other choice.

I planned on leaving after high school. Getting a football scholarship in another city with hundreds of thousands of people, where there were more streets than you could count on one hand. Coach said scouts would start coming to our football games now, to scope out the talent. And I wanted the talent to be me. I needed a one-way ticket out of here. More important, I wanted my dad to be at my games and witness it—witness me living out his dream like he intended.

Like she could sense my thoughts, Becca said, "Have you heard from your dad yet?"

I liked the way she asked that. There was no judgment. Unlike Jeff.

"Not yet," I said, turning off Main Street and onto a side road. The ground was gravel and we were bumping along. Becca opened her window and the humidity crept in, making my T-shirt stick to my skin. She didn't say anything else about the situation, which was for the best. I was over thinking about it.

I made a sharp left and pulled into a parking lot. There was a pharmacy, a convenience store, a post office, and—

"The old arcade?" Becca asked, leaning forward to look out the windshield. The sun was right above the building and we were both squinting.

"The old arcade," I said. A few of the neon letters had burned out, so the sign read ARC. From the outside, it looked run-down. There was no open sign or cars in the parking lot. Someone driving through town would think this place was a dive, that it had closed a decade ago. But they'd be wrong. And that was the cool thing about Crestmont. That it had all this secret charm that was known only to the people who grew up here. Like if you scraped off enough of the dirt, there'd be a shiny diamond waiting underneath.

"I haven't been here since I was a kid," Becca was saying to herself while we walked to the door. The town was so quiet today—there was no wind, no cars driving by. All I could hear was the crunch of gravel beneath our feet and the rustle of the paper bag Becca had gripped between her fingers.

I held the door open, we stepped inside, and the air-conditioning blasted us. It was one of the greatest feelings. We both stood there for a second, cooling down. Then I grabbed Becca's hand and pulled her through the second set of automatic doors and into the arcade. I didn't grab her hand for show either. There was no one here to lie to. I was starting to do it out of habit.

The arcade was exactly like I remembered it. Dimly lit, with rows and rows of games. There was the counter to our left, with a wall of prizes to trade tickets for. There were stuffed animals and plastic jewelry on display, and the air smelled like grease, popcorn, and a little like pot. I heard Becca gasp. Her eyes were wide open.

"I thought this place closed down years ago," she said, scanning the room. "I had my birthday party here when I was seven. I hit the jackpot on that *Wheel of Fortune* game."

Samson stood up from behind the counter then, eyes half-closed and red. Well, that explained the smell. "Wells?" he called, staring at the two of us.

"Hey, Sam." I walked to the counter and shook his hand. He looked older than he had last time I was here, more gray hair and wrinkles around his eyes. He was diagnosed with cancer a few years back and the arcade had closed while he was undergoing treatment. It reopened last summer when he was cancer free. I'd come in from time to time to check on it while he was in the hospital, make sure no kids were breaking in and playing without paying. I stopped coming by since the reopening. Until today.

"Feels like I 'aven't seen ya in years," he said, thick accent replacing all the *h*'s. Then his attention shifted over to Becca. "And 'o's this?"

She held out her hand. "Becca. It's nice to see you again. I had no idea this place was still open."

Samson nodded, pulling out two bags of tokens from under the counter and handing one to each of us. "It would 'ave closed if it weren't for this man right 'ere," he said, smiling at me. "You two 'ave the entire place to ya'selves. Enjoy." I paid for the tokens, thanked him, and followed Becca.

"What did he mean that this place would have closed without you?" Becca whispered when we were out of earshot. I briefly explained Samson's illness, but didn't really want to get into how I watched the place. Becca gave me this confused look, like she was trying to decipher a code or something, then walked right up to the racing game. There were two seats, red and blue, with matching steering wheels. She was eyeing the blue one.

"Let's play," I said, taking a seat on the red one. She sat down on the blue, slowly. "Something wrong?"

"I don't know how to drive."

I immediately started to laugh until I was doubled over, resting my head on the steering wheel. When I saw that she was being completely serious, glaring at me, I cleared my throat and straightened up.

"Oh. You're being serious?" She nodded. "This isn't like real driving, Becca. You'll be fine. Look." I grabbed her hands and placed them at ten and two on the wheel. "Spin it like this to turn right, then left. Yeah, just like that. The brake is the big one. Got it?"

She was concentrating so seriously. It was kind of cute.

"Brake is the big one," she repeated. "Got it. Put some tokens in. And Brett?"

I dropped in two tokens and hit the start button. "Yeah?"

"Don't let me win," she said, pointing a finger at my chest. "I mean it. Don't be all chivalrous. It's rude."

I tried to make sense of that. "You're saying being respectful is rude?"

She was staring at the screen, hands on the wheel. "In this situation, yes."

"Got it, ma'am."

The game started. Becca was horrible. She spent half of the first lap driving backward. When she managed to turn the car around, she was driving on the grass and running into buildings. She may have hit a person or two. Definitely a few mailboxes. It was physically painful for me to win each lap and not at least *try* to help her out but, like she said, chivalry is dead when it comes to gaming. So I finished that third lap with a smile on my face. I threw my fist in the air too. Just to show her how respectful and aware I was of her lack of talent.

"Jeez. You can tone it down a little," she grumbled, staring at the screen showing the match replay. It was footage of her hitting a tree.

We moved on to the next game. It was a huge wheel divided into different sections, each with a prize amount. The jackpot was one thousand tickets and the smallest was five. I spun it first—I was shocked the wheel didn't break because of how old it looked—and landed on one hundred. Becca went next. The arrow landed on five hundred. She pulled the tickets out happily, eyeing me the entire time with this smirk on her face, like she was making up for sucking at the racing game. I stuffed our tickets into my pocket and we moved on to the next game. This time, it was Skee-Ball. It was a large table with a ramp and holes in the upper half. Each had a different ticket amount. The point was to grab a ball, roll it across the table, and have it bounce into one of the different holes. The smaller the hole, the greater the prize.

"Let's make this interesting," I said, handing Becca the first ball. "If you get a ball in, you get to ask the other person a question. You said you wanted to get to know me better, right? Here's your chance."

"So this is like the Skee-Ball version of twenty questions?"

"Something like that, yeah."

Becca nodded, squaring her shoulders and cracking her neck. "Let's do this." She rolled the first ball and into the hole it went. The smallest one too, right in the middle.

I whistled, watching her grin spread. "Impressive. Ask away."

She sat on the edge of the ramp, glancing up at me. "What's your connection with this place? You seem really close with Samson," she said, nodding toward the counter.

"I worked here when I was fifteen, just for the summer," I explained.

"But I thought your family . . ." *Was rich*, was what she meant but didn't say. She looked uncomfortable, chewing on her lip.

I shrugged, gesturing for her to stand so I could take my turn. "My family is well off, sure. But this was my favorite place as a kid. It was the only real time my dad and I spent together that didn't involve a football. So when I saw that Sam needed the help, I volunteered. He couldn't pay me for most weeks so I just played the games for free and ate loads of popcorn. It was pretty sweet." I rolled the ball, missed, and handed the next one to Becca. She was giving me that confused, who-are-you face again. "Your turn."

She blinked, said, "Right," and took the ball. When she rolled it, she missed.

My ball landed in the five-hundred-point hole next. "Favorite color?" I asked.

She thought about it for a second. "All of them. Undecided." She rolled and scored. "Favorite food?"

"Burgers," I said. "And fries."

I rolled. Missed. Becca rolled. Scored.

"How old were you when you had your first kiss?" she asked.

"Thirteen. It was during recess and we both had braces." I rolled again and scored this time. "Are you and your mom close?"

She smiled, bending to grab another ball. "Yeah. She's my best friend." Becca rolled and missed, passing me the next ball. I scored.

"What were you thinking before when I said I used to work here?" I asked. "You had this funny look on your face."

Becca grabbed a ball and tossed it between two hands, her eyes following it. "Nothing. Just that, I don't know, you're different than I thought you'd be."

"How so?"

"Like, you're easy to talk to," she began, "and attractive people are *never* easy to talk to. That's a scientific fact."

"You think I'm—"

"And you're really nice," she continued, ignoring me. "Working here and checking in on the place when Samson was sick. I mean, I kind of knew that already. Everyone at Eastwood always goes on about how nice you are and stuff. But it's different, to see it firsthand. Am I rambling? I feel like I'm rambling."

I was smiling by the time she finished talking.

"Not rambling," I lied.

"Good." She said it like she knew I was lying and picked up the next ball. She scored again. One hundred points. "Do you regret this?" she asked. "Our fake relationship."

I didn't even have to think about it. "No," I said. "Not at all."

It was starting to feel normal, being around Becca. Was it rude for me to be surprised by how much I was enjoying her company? Because I was enjoying it. I felt comfortable around her in this way I never had before. It was like we had skipped the beginning awkward phase when you first meet someone and aren't entirely sure if you can act like yourself around them. I guess jumping straight into dating could do that to two people. With Becca, I felt like I could be myself.

There was this kindness about her and this intelligence too, like she understood more than she let on. It was nice.

"Me either." She said it shyly. It reminded me of how she looked that day in the hall after I kissed her.

I picked up the last ball and missed. It sucked too, because I had the perfect question. I'd save it for later.

It took us an hour to go through all our tokens. When we had, I bought more. We stayed in the arcade until we couldn't hold any more tickets in our pockets or hands. I started looping mine through my belt and they trailed behind when I walked. Becca found this hilarious, picking off a few when she thought I wasn't looking and adding them to her own stash. When we were done, we combined our tickets for a total of two thousand and traded them in for three prizes: a red plastic ring with a rose on it, a pack of sour gummy worms, and a stuffed blue whale.

Becca took the ring, we shared the worms, and the whale was undecided.

We were sitting outside on the parking lot's curb, knee to knee, under the sun. It was cooler now, and the leaves on the trees were blowing in the breeze. Becca's hair was whipping around her face, constantly going into my eyes. After I ate the last gummy worm, she hauled out the brown paper bag—where had she kept it this entire time?—and placed it on my knee.

"What's the verdict?" I asked, eyeing the bag. "Did you have fun today? Am I allowed to finally eat whatever that is?"

She laughed, pulled her knees to her chest, and said, "You can eat them."

I grabbed the bag, stood up, did a little victory dance, then sat back down and ripped the bag open. There were four little balls inside, all covered in white sugar. They were the same ones I had bought for my mom and, holy shit, they smelled incredible. I reached in and grabbed one. By some miracle, it was still warm. How was that possible?

"My mom calls them jelly bells," she explained, grabbing one for herself. "It's fried dough stuffed with strawberry jelly and covered in sugar. It was the first recipe she really perfected when she started baking. They were originally called jelly balls but, since they're my favorite and my mom calls me Bells, she renamed them."

I was listening, I really was, but I was also starving and these things smelled like literal heaven and I really thought I'd drop dead if I didn't eat one in the next second.

When Becca took a bite, I shoved the whole thing in my mouth. I may have moaned because this was definitely one of the best things I'd ever eaten.

"Remember when you asked what my favorite food was?" I asked, a cloud of white powder spewing from my mouth. Becca nodded. There was sugar all over her mouth. "I change my answer to these."

We sat there while the sun began to set, eating the rest. When we were both covered in powder, we dusted ourselves off and I drove Becca home. She was talking about the games, replaying which were her favorite and why. She kept toying with the rose ring on her finger. The blue whale was sitting on the dashboard. When I pulled into her apartment building, she sat there for a minute in silence, staring at the sky. I wanted to ask what she was thinking, but I kept quiet.

After a moment, she turned to me and said, "You're lucky, Brett, to have a family like yours. Not because of the money. Just having two parents that are there for you and are these role models of what love should look like. And I don't want to overstep, but I don't think you should be upset at your dad for missing your football game. It was just one game. Try to think of the hundreds of games he's been to, all right? All those times he put in the effort to support you—that's what matters, not the one time he failed."

Then she got out of the car, waved goodbye, and left.

I sat there for a while thinking about how I had lucked out on choosing a pretty great fake girlfriend.

Becca

MY MOM WAS SITTING AT the kitchen table when I walked inside. The oven was on, she had an apron tied around her neck, and our apartment smelled like vanilla—the three signs that she was beginning a new recipe.

"How was your day?" she asked, glancing over her shoulder and smiling at me.

"Good." I grabbed a water bottle from the fridge and leaned against the counter.

"What did you and Cassandra do?"

I felt a little twinge of guilt for telling my mom I was spending the day at Cassie's house, helping her fill out college applications. Some lies were for the greater good, though. Like escaping another Brett fiasco.

"Nothing. Just college stuff," I answered, looking anywhere but her eyes. My mom (all moms?) had this talent of knowing exactly when I was lying. It's like she could see it on my face or something. The trick was to say as little as possible and make a hasty exit. I was nearly out of the kitchen, almost to safety, when she called my name.

"I was talking to Cara on the phone before you walked in!" I froze, slowly turned around, and saw That Look on her face. Nothing good could come out of her talking to Cassie's mom. "She invited us over for dinner tonight. I told her that was so funny, because you were already *at* her house. And you know what she said?"

I shook my head. Braced for impact.

"Cara said," she continued, "that you weren't there."

I choked out a laugh. "That is very funny, Mom. You know how bad her eyesight is. Come to think of it, I don't think she was wearing her glasses at all today. And Cassie and I spent the entire day in her bedroom, so it's possible she didn't even see—"

"Becca."

I unraveled like a spool of string.

"Fine! I wasn't with Cassie." I sank down in the chair across from her, defeated, and let the truth spill out. "I was with Brett," I mumbled under my breath.

I didn't know it was physically possible for my mother's

83

face to go from upset to unbelievably happy in under one second. Now she was beaming. She was even sitting up straighter, leaning across the table.

"The boy from the bakery?" She whispered it like Brett was in the other room eavesdropping.

"Yes."

"What did you two do?" She said it calmly. Casually. I appreciated that she was at least *trying* to restrain herself. I told her about the arcade (she was equally surprised it was still open), and about the jelly bells, which, yes, Mom, Brett loved. Duh. And no, Mom, I do not like him like that. We are friends. At point I could see her about to bubble over—she was bouncing in her seat—so I needed to leave the room ASAP.

"Can we postpone the interrogation till tomorrow? I need to study for my calculus test."

The timer on the stove went off and she slipped on a pair of oven mitts. And, oh my god, it smelled amazing. I almost decided to continue the interrogation right then just to eat whatever was creating that heavenly smell.

"Speaking of tomorrow," my mom said, placing a toothpick into a muffin and nodding when it came out dry, "I need you to pick up a shift in the morning. Don't give me that face, Becca. It's just an hour or two to help open the store, then you can come home and study."

"Moooooooom," I groaned.

"I'll make you fresh jelly bells for school on Monday morning. Feel free to share them with whoever you choose," she added, winking. No doubt a not-so-subtle reference to Brett.

I caved anyway. It was the power of the jelly bells. "Fine. But two hours and then I'm out of there. Promise?"

"Promise."

I retreated to my room, snuck back into the kitchen ten minutes later and stole a muffin, which, honestly, changed my life, then actually began studying like I should have done two days ago. Having a fake boyfriend may have been a little exciting, but I wasn't about to stop being a straight-A student, especially with college applications coming up. I still had no idea what I even wanted to do. The only thing I really liked was reading. Maybe I'd study English litera- ture. Or creative writing. Half the time I told myself I'd take a year off like Cassie, stay home and help my mom out with the bakery, and then figure out this whole college thing later. If I didn't score a scholarship to help my mom with tuition, I wasn't sure I'd even be able to go to college at all.

But as long as I was out of high school, that was what mattered.

It wasn't even like I really hated high school or anything. I mean, I disliked it the average teenage amount, but it just felt like Crestmont was this little part of the world and there was so much more out there to be seen. And I wanted to explore more than just the blue lockers of Eastwood High.

When I was in my pajamas, lying in bed with the lights off, my phone rang. I glanced at the screen, lowered the brightness after it burned my eyes, and saw a text from Brett. It was a selfie of him lying in bed with his eyes closed, pretending to be asleep.

Another text came right after. *Dreaming of jelly bells,* it read.

I smiled, placed the rose ring on my nightstand, and went to sleep.

My mom and I had a routine for opening up the bakery. She handled the kitchen—warming up the ovens, making the cupcake batter, unfreezing the cannoli shells—while I set up the rest of the place. I unstacked the chairs, wiped down the tables and counters, did another quick sweep of the floors, made sure the register had change, and, when it was eight o'clock, flipped over the open sign and unlocked the door. This morning there were two women waiting outside right on the hour. They each had an order waiting for pickup. I called out to let Mom know.

Sunday was the busiest day at the bakery. Mom said it was because of Sunday dinners and how families all got together, had a huge meal, and ordered pastries for dessert. I was kind of jealous that people did that. Both my parents were only children, so I had no cousins, no aunts or uncles— nothing. My mom's parents both died when I was a kid. I could remember attending each of their funerals and my parents not letting me see the bodies. I was too young, was what they said. My dad's parents were still alive, but they retired and moved down to Florida years ago. Not that it matters. I doubt they'd want to see me either.

My mom came out with the women's orders and they were on their way. She was also holding a stack of pink papers in her hand. I took a closer look when she placed them on the counter, in front of the cash register. They were flyers for the bakery. Promotional flyers.

"Mom," I said slowly, lifting one of them up. "What's this for?"

"Business has been a little quiet lately, Bells. Try to hand those out to customers, will you? Get the word out around town."

Under the Hart's Cupcakes logo, in small black text, it said, "Try a Free Cannoli with Any Purchase." "We're handing out free stuff now?"

My mom wasn't listening. She was bustling around, wiping nonexistent crumbs off the counter.

"Mom." I grabbed her hand, looked her in the eye.

"What is it with these flyers? Is business okay? Is there something you're not telling me?"

"Becca," she said, reaching out and adjusting my apron. She was smiling that don't-worry-about-it, everything-is-going-to-be-okay smile. "I'm simply trying out a new strategy to bring in business. That's it, hon. Don't worry yourself. We're *fine*. Will you try to hand a few of them out? Place them in the bags with the customers' orders."

I let out a breath. "Fine, Mom." She blew me a kiss and disappeared into the back. I didn't read too much into it. If she said everything was fine, then everything was fine.

I pulled out my calculus textbook and began studying. Every minute helped. I was halfway through a chapter on exponents when the bell chimed. I closed my textbook, plastered on my best employee smile, looked up, and immediately froze. It was Jenny, walking up to the counter, eyes on me.

"My brother placed an order for this morning," she said, crossing her arms over her chest. She was wearing a baby-pink denim jacket that was way too warm for weather like this.

"What name is the order under?" I asked, pulling out the sheet.

"Parker."

I scanned the list, crossed off his name, called out to

my mom, and then tapped my fingers awkwardly on the counter.

"It'll be a minute," I said, opening up my textbook because I had nothing else to do.

Jenny nodded, eyes scanning the bakery. "Your family owns this?" she asked. Right. Our friendship ended before the bakery opened.

"My mom does."

"How's Brett?" she asked curiously.

It was weird. The tables had turned. I was the one with the boyfriend now.

"He's fine," I finally answered.

Silence stretched on. I wanted to sink into a hole and never return.

Jenny picked up one of the flyers. Playing with the corners, she said, "You could have told me you were dating someone. Even though we're not close anymore . . . you still could have told me. I would have wanted to know." She sniffled, cleared her throat, and held up the flyer. "What is this?"

It took me a second to respond, a second to understand what she had just said and brushed aside. "Mom's trying to bring in new business," I said.

"'Try a free cannoli with any purchase,'" Jenny read. "Does that start today?"

I shrugged. "Guess so."

A century later, my mother walked in with Jenny's order and whispered "Flyers" to me before leaving. I tried my best to sneak one in the bag but Jenny caught me midway.

"To spread the word," I grumbled, holding out the bag for her. Her eyes traveled from my face to the flyer and back again. The seconds dragged on.

Then she grabbed an entire stack of flyers, shoved them into her purse, and left without another word.

"Was that Jennifer?" my mom asked, reappearing when the door shut.

"Yeah."

"Wow. She looks so different. Are you two still friends?"

I could vividly remember telling her about my friendship breakup with Jenny. But that was also after the summer she opened the bakery, so she had other things on her mind.

"Not anymore."

My mom nodded, patted my shoulder, said, "She took the flyers. Told you it would work!" then disappeared into the back. To be fair, it wasn't a guaranteed success. For all I knew, we could have just witnessed paper theft. My mom didn't seem to care, though. I could hear the whiz of the blender and reopened my textbook to continue studying.

The two hours flew by. Thankfully there were no more Eastwood High student sightings, and as soon as the clock struck ten, I made my escape. I was walking home with my headphones in when my feet did that thing again, where they took me somewhere completely different than the place I'd originally intended to go.

I walked down Main Street and took a left at the intersection. It was hotter than normal, and I tied my hair up to keep it from sticking to my neck. Another right turn and I was standing on my dad's street. His house looked the same. Except for a new sign on the lawn. It was a big pink stork, holding a swaddled baby. Before I knew it, I was standing on the sidewalk, reading the *Congratulations* message. His daughter's name was Penelope. I had a sister. Half sister. All those years of being an only child flashed through my mind. I stumbled on the sidewalk. My knee scraped against the concrete. I felt the blood begin to trickle down my skin.

A sister.

A pair of white sneakers appeared. There was a woman staring down at me, face creased with worry. Her mouth was moving but I couldn't hear a word. All I could focus on was her stomach, flatter than before.

"Are you all right?" my dad's new wife (or was it girlfriend?) asked, holding out her hand. I noticed the ring. Wife.

I stood up on my own and brushed the dirt off my clothes. "I'm fine," I said, the same second both our eyes drifted to my knee, which was covered in blood and loose pieces of cement.

"I'll grab you a Band-Aid and a warm towel." She walked up the driveway, pausing to look over her shoulder when she reached the porch. "Follow me," she said, stepping inside and leaving the door open.

I walked up the steps in a daze. I was thinking that she must know who I am. Why else would she invite a complete stranger into her home? My second thought was that, oh my god, what if he was home? I noticed the empty driveway for the first time. Thankfully, his car was gone.

I kept walking, my feet hovering on the doorstep. I felt that familiar feeling of guilt twist inside me. I was imagining my mom and what she would say if she knew I was here, about to walk into his house. It felt like a betrayal of her. It always did. But there, right beside the guilt, was so much curiosity. I just wanted a glimpse into his life. One little peek. And then maybe that would be enough. Maybe then I'd never return.

I stepped inside.

All the walls were blue. It looked like someone grabbed a handful of the sky and threw it everywhere. There were framed photos covering nearly every inch of empty space. Most were of my dad and his new wife, smiling at the camera with sunlight in their eyes. A few were of their baby.

She had big brown eyes and a little dimple in her cheek. It was like a shrine to his new life. Where were the photos of me? The other family he had for twelve years? How could my mother and I spend the last five years trying to piece our lives back together while he was here, rebuilding his so easily?

His wife returned, holding a towel. I wanted to ask her name. How they met. When they got married. Did they know each other before the divorce?

"Here," she said, "use this to wipe off the blood." I had this weird thought that she'd use it for DNA testing to find out who I was, but grabbed the towel anyway because that was ridiculous.

The cut stung when I pressed the cloth to it. I wiped off my leg and noticed how quiet it was. There was no baby crying. No radio or television noises in the background. My mom always kept the radio on, even when no one was home. Now my skin was starting to crawl, and I felt weird and dirty all over. I wanted to get out of here. Fast. I kept picturing my dad's car pulling into the driveway and the moment he would step inside. What would it be like? Watching his two worlds collide?

"What's your name?" the woman asked, holding out a Band-Aid.

I guess she really didn't know who I was. Made sense.

My mom and I clearly weren't important to my father.

"Cassie," I said. She smiled. I noticed the small gap between her front teeth and the way she blew her curls out of her eyes. And I hated it. I wanted her to be rude. Or have some flaw that would make it easy to dislike her. Instead she seemed nice. Really nice, the type of person who hands out Band-Aids to strangers.

"Do you live around here?" she asked.

I shook my head. Took a step back. The guilt was twisting higher, reaching my lungs, making it hard to breathe. This felt wrong. So wrong. I mumbled a goodbye and left, ran down the driveway while scanning the street like a crazy person. I was a few houses down when I swear I heard someone call my name. I didn't look back. I kept running until I was inside my apartment, out of breath. I locked the doors, locked everyone out, and sank onto the floor with my knees to my chest. I shut my eyes and waited for my heart rate to slow down.

I thought I'd feel different.

I thought this would feel better.

Instead I was even more confused.

Their house seemed normal. There was nothing special about it. Nothing extravagant. His wife seemed nice. But my mom was nice too. He had a daughter now. But he had me before. So why swap out one for another? I thought going there would give me answers, not more questions.

I groaned, stood up, and sulked to my room. I shouldn't have done that. I should have gone straight home and minded my business.

Even though my dad lived a few streets over, it felt like a different world. And I should have kept it that way. I shouldn't have let the worlds collide. And if my mother found out . . . Would she be hurt? Betrayed? Would she think this life with her wasn't enough for me? Because it was. It so was. But five years wondering why is a long time, and wanting answers to questions I'm unable to ask makes it even harder.

My heart was beginning to hurt, the same way it did the day he left. It was slow at first, a subtle burn. And then the flames began to grow, devouring everything in their path. So I did the only thing I could think of. I grabbed a book. Any book. I didn't even bother reading the title. I flipped to the last chapter because I needed the happy ending right now. I read and read and read until reality faded into fiction.

Brett

ME AND MY MOM WERE waiting on the porch Sunday morning when the taxi parked outside our house. My dad stepped out, smile on his face, luggage in hand. I ran down the steps to help. He patted my back, asked about the football game, and apologized for not coming back on time. I thought back to what Becca said after the arcade, to remember all the games he attended. I told him it was okay, that we won anyway, and we walked up the driveway. I was grinning now, happiest when my whole family was home.

We had dinner together that night. My mom ordered food from my dad's favorite restaurant. She was being really quiet during the meal, hardly eating. I asked her a few times if she was all right and she'd pat my hand and nod. I asked my dad question after question about his time in New York: What did he do? Did he go to Central Park? He said he was too busy with business to sightsee. Which made sense.

When he said he had to leave again next weekend, my mom dropped her glass of wine onto the table. It spilled everywhere, staining the white tablecloth red. We all froze for a second before she ran off into the kitchen, returning with a roll of paper towels. She was crying, hands shaking, and she wouldn't stop apologizing under her breath. My dad grabbed her hands and they walked away together. I heard the door to their bedroom shut. It was weird. Really weird.

I grabbed a towel and cleaned the table. I put all the food away and brought my dad's luggage upstairs. The door to their room was still closed. I could hear them whispering. My dad was apologizing for being away so much. "I'm doing this for us," he was saying. I could hear my mom crying still. I knew it was hard on her when he left, and he'd been leaving more often than usual in the past few months. It started off as a weekend here and there. Lately, it had been almost every weekend. It was hard on her. It was hard on me. But he always came back. Wasn't that what mattered?

When my parents stopped talking, I ran back to my room before they opened the door and caught me eavesdropping. I felt weird having to tiptoe around my own house. My parents never kept secrets before. My mom never acted that way on the rare occasion she spilled a drink. We always stayed up laughing when my dad came home. This was a first.

I lay in bed, waiting for my dad to knock. He always brought me back something from his trips. Last time it was a hat from Chicago. Before that a watch from Washington and a key chain from North Carolina.

This time he brought back nothing.

Another first.

It rained the next day. The sky was gray all morning, thunder beating through. Becca made a huge deal about having to eat lunch in the cafeteria. She was moping the whole time, even when I cleared a table in the corner for the two of us. Sure, people were staring, but I ignored them. When she pulled a book out of her bag and started to read, I didn't question it. I was stuck in my own head too.

My mom was acting strange this morning before I left for school. She was still in bed when I woke up. My mom *never* slept in later than eight. I peeked my head through the door to ask if she needed anything, make sure she was okay after last night. She said she was fine. I didn't believe it. I left anyway to pick up Becca.

My dad was back in town now. Things were supposed

to be going back to normal. Instead, it felt like something was off. And the worst part was that, whatever it was, my parents were keeping it a secret.

"What are you reading?" I asked Becca to distract myself. Without taking her eyes off the book, she shushed me. "Come ooooooooon. Show me."

She kept ignoring me.

"Just one little peek. Please?"

Her eyes remained locked on her book.

I reached out, quick as lightning, and grabbed it from her hands.

If looks could kill.

"Brett! Give it back!" She was in a bad mood. Like, very bad. I was kind of scared. But I really wanted to know what this book was about.

"*The Last Song*," I read aloud. I flipped through the pages, read the synopsis, did it one more time just to be annoying (what was up with me today?), then handed it back to Becca. "Is it any good?"

She ripped it from my hands a little too aggressively. "Yes."

"Can I ask you a question?"

"No."

"You know, Becca, I'm having a pretty rough morning and my girlfriend being mad at me is not helping."

Now she looked up, ever so slowly, and shut the book.

"What happened?" she asked. Then Becca looked around the cafeteria, as if just remembering we were inside, surrounded by people, and shrank down in her seat a little.

For a brief moment, I considered not telling her. Whatever it was that my parents were going through, it felt weird to admit it out loud. It was like lifting up a curtain and finding a huge mess hiding behind. But then Becca was sitting there, in the middle of the cafeteria she hated, giving up her lunch to be with me, and what else could I do but tell her the truth? She looked like she genuinely cared, like that moment in the car after the arcade. And maybe she did care. Maybe I could trust her to help me figure this out.

So I told her about the weird dinner last night, the whispered conversation my parents had, my dad not bringing me home anything from New York, and then about my mom this morning. She didn't roll her eyes and say I was overreacting. She didn't get angry like Jeff did, saying I looked up to my dad too much. She didn't make me feel like a baby for being hurt that my parents were keeping something from me. Instead she reached across the table and held my hand. And I didn't think it was for show either. It was only for me this time.

"That is a little weird. Did you ask your mom?"

I told her that no, I hadn't. "She was half asleep when I

left this morning. And she seems kind of sad. I don't want to make it worse."

Becca was nodding, eyebrows creased in the middle. She was really paying attention.

"I don't think you should read too much into it. It was one weird night. Right? Wait and see what happens before you start to freak out."

Easier said than done. I was already nearing freak-out zone.

"What you need is to distract yourself," she continued, picking up her book. "Reading helps me. It's like I'm in another world when I read. And all the problems in my life don't exist anymore. It helps." Then, realizing she'd said something sort of personal, she started to blush. "You need something to distract yourself with."

Being so caught up in my own problems, I didn't realize that something was bothering her this morning too. She wasn't *just* mad. What did she need distracting from?

"What did you do yesterday?"

Becca picked up her book again. "Helped my mom at the bakery and studied for calc."

"That's it?"

"That's it."

She wouldn't look up from her book.

I polished off my burger and Becca had flipped through

101

a couple of pages when Jeff slid into the seat beside me. There was water dripping off his hair and clothes, soaking the table and forming a puddle on the floor. "Forgot my lunch in the car," he explained, pulling a half-squished sandwich out of his pocket. He shook his hair out like a dog. Water sprayed everywhere. Becca shrieked and quickly hid her book under the table.

I elbowed him in the ribs.

"What?" Lettuce hung out of his mouth.

"What are you doing?" I asked.

"Having lunch with my best friend and his girlfriend."

I glanced at Becca. She was eyeing Jeff like he was of an alien species.

"Becca," I said slowly, "this is Jeff. Jeff, Becca." He smiled again, lettuce everywhere, and Becca slowly placed her book back on the table.

"You're in my calc class," she said.

"Think so." Crumbs fell from his mouth. "Think you failed that test today?"

Doubt it. She'd been studying for a week.

"Aced it," Becca said. I felt kind of proud, like yeah, my girlfriend is smart as hell and happy to own it. Then remembered that wait, she's not my girlfriend. Still proud, though.

"You two coming to the marsh party this Friday?" Jeff asked once he finished eating.

I smacked myself a little because I'd forgotten to tell Becca about that. It completely slipped my mind with everything that happened this weekend.

"What's a marsh party?" she asked.

I explained how bordering Crestmont and the neighboring town was Lovers' Lake. How it used to be two separate lakes but the water levels changed over the years, and how the strip of land separating them started to shrink. Now they met in the middle, and it sort of looked like two broken pieces of a heart. At the edge of the lake was a marsh, which was just a huge grassy area covered in water before it stretched into the forest. After the second football game of the season, the team and a bunch of seniors would spend the night there, celebrating. It was a bit of a tradition at Eastwood High.

"It's this Friday," Jeff cut in. "The whole team's going."

I watched Becca's face, waiting for some type of sign. She was nodding, thinking. Did she hate it? Did it sound cool? Would she go with me? To be honest, I'd go without her. I'd been looking forward to this since sophomore year and I wasn't about to miss it because she'd rather stay home and read. Then I regretted thinking that because it was kind of rude. But really, would she come? It would be fun. And even with this fake relationship, our worlds had stayed separate. I mean, this was the first time she'd spoken to one of my friends. I was curious what would happen if our two worlds overlapped a little more.

"Lovers' Lake," she repeated. "Why haven't I heard of that?"

"The real name is Crestmont Lake," Jeff explained. "Kids started calling it Lovers' Lake because of, you know, the things that happen there."

Becca was blinking, totally not understanding. "What kind of things?"

"Like . . ." Jeff's mouth was hanging open like a fish, and he turned to me, looking a little mortified. "Take it away, Wells."

"He's saying people go there to hook up," I explained, laughing when she choked on her water. "It's a lake in the middle of the woods, Becca. It's dark and private and Crestmont is boring as hell. You gotta make fun out of what you can."

"It can get a little crazy," Jeff added, a little too enthusiastically.

And then, by some miracle, Becca said the last thing I expected. "Okay. Sounds fun."

Jeff pumped his fist in the air, screamed, "Hell yeah! Knew you'd be in," then reached into his bag and took out a little white box. Becca spotted it the same time I did. She leaned across the table so quickly she knocked her water bottle over.

"Is that . . ."

Jeff opened the box and, to both of our shock, pulled out a jelly bell. He ate it with his eyes closed, making this uncomfortable moaning sound.

When he opened his eyes, he stared between the two of us. "What?"

"That's a jelly bell," Becca said.

"And?"

"You went to my mom's bakery," she said, dumbfounded.

"Your mom owns that place? That's cool. Jenny was handing out flyers to the team during lunch. Thought I'd swing by and take up that free cannoli offer. That place is *amazing*. . . . Why are you staring at me like that?"

Becca's mouth was literally hanging open. "Jenny handed out flyers?" she said.

Jeff looked at me. "What is going on?" I shrugged. Hell if I knew. He pulled a pink crumpled ball out of his pocket and smoothed it down on the table. It was a flyer for Hart's Cupcakes. Becca picked it up, held it to her face like she was conducting a scientific analysis.

"Jenny gave you this?" she said again.

"Yes." Jeff gave me a look, picked up his bag, and left.

I turned to Becca, who still looked dazed. "What's going on?"

"Don't you think it's weird?" she said. "Jenny handing out flyers to my mom's bakery?"

I shrugged. "Maybe."

She nodded to herself. "Very weird."

I steered the conversation back on track. "You don't really have to come to the party if you don't want to."

She carefully folded the flyer into a square and put it in her pocket. "I don't mind," she said, now looking at me. "And it'll be good for people to see us out together somewhere other than your football games. Make this seem more real."

Sometimes I actually forgot that we were supposed to be dating. Our friendship already felt so normal. I reached across the table and grabbed her hand then, just in case.

"I think people are buying it," I said. "My teammates haven't said a word. Even Jeff hasn't doubted it. Back to Lovers' Lake, I didn't think you'd say yes."

"It's not my usual scene, sure, but it sounds sort of fun. And it's not like I'll be awkwardly alone. You'll be there, and you're pretty good company."

"*Pretty* good?"

"Definitely above average."

"I'll have you know I'm somewhat of a hot commodity in these halls, Hart."

"Then lucky me for being the one dating you. Now tell me"—she lowered her voice, leaned across the table—"ever brought a girl to Lovers' Lake?"

I leaned in too, until our noses were almost touching.

"No," I said. "You'll be the first."

Becca

LOVERS' LAKE WAS DISGUSTING.

And crowded. And it smelled horrible.

I was trying to remember how I allowed Brett to drag me here when he tugged on my hand, pulling me forward. Yes, we were wading through grass that was covered in murky water and yes, I was purposely trying to keep my mind preoccupied with anything other than this disgusting lake/marsh/whatever-the-hell-it-was I was currently attempting to walk through. I could hear voices and see some sort of light farther down. Definitely not a fire. It was too wet. Maybe a flashlight? That would be nice. Let's illuminate all the bugs circling my head.

"Stop pulling me!" I hissed, tugging back on Brett's arm. "I'm going to trip and drown."

"The water's not even a foot deep, Becca."

Whatever!

We kept walking. It was dark. Like dark enough that the moon seemed to be ten times brighter than normal. There were people walking behind us and a few in front, leading the way. Brett introduced me to them when we first arrived. I tried my best to remember their names, I really did, but one step into this mushy grass had me forgetting everything other than my new white Converse, which were currently being destroyed.

I still wasn't entirely sure what Lovers' Lake was. And it was way too dark for me to make out my surroundings. All I knew was that Brett had driven down a bumpy pathway—I flew into the window a few times—until we came to a clearing where dozens of other cars were parked. It looked like all the grass had been crushed by tires so many times it just gave up trying to regrow. That wasn't the end of the journey, though. After we exited the car, we had to walk through this path in the forest and my life was left in the hands of Brett (literally) and whichever teenager with a flashlight was leading us to Lovers' Lake.

For the record, my expectations weren't high.

I could not believe people willingly came here for fun. Let alone took their clothes off and did whatever else in the trees. I kept glancing around and shuddering. I wanted to take a shower just thinking about it. Plus, the marsh had that weird fishy smell that fills the air after it rains and there were bugs flying everywhere. It was too dark to see them—which may have been a good thing—but they were buzzing in my ears and I kept imagining one flying right into my brain. The bottom half of my legs were covered in mosquito bites (partially my fault for wearing shorts). All in all, it reminded me of the summer when my family, pre-divorce, went camping. We didn't even last the first night. After the tent collapsed, we packed up all our stuff and left.

I checked my phone and saw it was almost eleven. I couldn't believe the night hadn't even started yet! My curfew was one, but I suspected my mother would be okay with me coming home late as long as Brett was the one dropping me off.

The people in front of us started to cheer then, and I peeked around Brett's back to find the narrow path opening into a clearing. Thank god. I could have cried on the spot. I had no idea what to expect, maybe some blankets or some sort of organized structure for people to sit on. Instead there were fallen tree trunks rearranged in a square, a few lawn chairs, and flashlights dangling off of branches to light up the area. People were sitting around drinking, leaning against trees, splashing each other with muddy water and, yes, as Jeff said, sneaking off into the surrounding forest.

It was all very high school. Meaning it was both completely gross and a weird kind of cool.

Brett let go of my hand when he spotted his teammates. They'd won their second football game tonight, and he spent the entire ride over replaying every moment out loud, as if I wasn't sitting in the first row of the bleachers watching. The upside was that I was slowly learning football lingo. (My vocabulary had surpassed "touchdown.")

I also noticed that his parents weren't at the game. Again. I tried to ask him about it and he mumbled something about his dad having just left for Ohio. *Two missed games in a row*, I added to my mental tally. This wasn't looking good. Brett, on the other hand, was looking great. That smile on his face could fool anyone. It hadn't left since his team won. It was weird, because he'd been kind of moping around at school this week. He didn't talk about it much, but I knew his parents were weighing him down. Especially since they'd missed this game too. But now? In this clearing? He was the normal Brett Wells that everyone loved. One-hundred-watt smile and all.

So, sure, I'd go along with it. Tonight we'd be Brett and

Becca: The Couple. We already had the hand-holding part down. Even the couple bantering. And I'd yet to take one glance at the book in my bag. The night was off to a good start.

If only I could find somewhere to sit so I could take my feet out of this grass/water situation.

I was eyeing one of the tree logs. There was a puddle separating me from it. It looked pretty shallow. But it was wide, stretching right into the trees lining each side of the narrow clearing. Long too. There was no way I could jump across. Maybe if I got a running start . . .

Brett appeared beside me and bent over, nearly knocking me backward. I yelled his name, waved my arms at my sides like a windmill to stay upright. He spun around and caught me. It was those football player reflexes. And he was smiling. Always smiling.

"Sorry," he said then, hands still on my hips. His hair was wet somehow, and a drop of water was slowly trailing down his nose. "I was trying to give you a piggyback ride across the puddle." He turned around again, bent over, and reached behind to pat his back. "Hop on." I only had to glance down at my white sneakers for a second before deciding that this was a no-brainer. I wrapped my arms around his neck and in one swift motion Brett hooked his hands behind my knees and lifted me onto his back. I felt like a kid being carried through the puddle, water splashing up on either side. Brett pretended to almost tip over—at this point I had a death grip on his neck—then slowly let me down where the grass was dry.

"I'm gonna get a drink. Want something?" he asked. I shook my head and he disappeared.

I was looking around for a friendly face when I spotted Jenny standing on her own, leaning against a tree. I took a deep breath and walked over, careful to watch where I was stepping.

"Hey," I said, waving.

"Becca," she replied, sipping from her cup.

"I just wanted to say thank you." She looked confused, so I added, "For handing out those flyers for my mom's bakery? Jeff told me you gave some to the football team. That was cool of you."

She shrugged, eyes scanning the trees. "It was no big deal. The pastries were really good and you know how much the football team eats. . . ."

Well, I didn't, but I could imagine.

"Anyway," I said, "thanks again."

I started to walk away, then stopped, remembering what she had said in the bakery.

"I didn't think we were friends anymore," I blurted out, turning around.

She looked kind of stunned. "What?"

"That's why I didn't tell you about Brett. I didn't think you would care. Or even want to know. And I didn't *want* to tell you, Jenny. You always mocked me for being single, you made me feel horrible about it. So why would I want to share this with you?"

"I . . . I didn't know I made you feel like that."

"Well, you did."

She was staring at her cup, kicking her foot in the dirt. It was weird to see her not looking confident like usual. "Is it too late for me to apologize?"

"Maybe," I said. "But if you keep handing out those flyers for my mom, maybe we can call it even."

Jenny smiled. "Maybe."

She held up her cup in a mock cheers and I took another step in the right direction, heading back over to the tree bench, and took a seat. Brett appeared a second later, kissed my cheek, and sat beside me. His hand immediately went to my knee. I reminded myself this was what couples did. This was what Brett expected me to do.

I placed my hand on top of his.

"Talking with Jenny?" he said, sounding surprised. "What's that about?"

I glanced at her again, standing by herself in the trees. I knew what that felt like, to be the outsider looking in. But Jenny had never been an outsider . . . so where were all her friends?

I met Brett's eyes and smiled. "We were talking about you," I said, "and why I let you bring me into this mess. I don't get the hype. At all. This is really gross. My shoes are destroyed and my legs are covered in bug bites."

"I told you not to wear shorts," he said.

"You told me when I was already wearing them!"

His shoulders shook as he laughed. Brett had this contagious laugh. It was loud and booming and demanded attention. Kind of like him.

"I like the shorts," he said. Pause. "You look nice."

He was sitting too close to me and I was wondering how he still managed to smell so freaking good in the grossest situations. He smelled like cinnamon, kind of warm. Then I started to think about this cinnamon cake my mom used to bake. It was my favorite before the jelly bells. Then I was thinking about the selfie Brett sent me of him lying in bed that night after the arcade.

I blinked. Pulled myself together. We were already in dangerous waters, literally, and I did not need this fake relationship messing with my feelings, blurring what was and wasn't real.

This, I reminded myself, was not.

"You've been looking forward to this for how long?" I asked him.

"Three years," Brett answered. "Me and Jeff tried to sneak in during sophomore year. We waited until the game ended and followed the seniors through the forest. We thought we were so smart, that we'd get away with it. No luck."

Jeff, appearing out of nowhere, sat on my left and effortlessly joined the conversation. "It was like they could smell the sophomore on us. We barely made it out of my truck before they kicked us out."

"You two are so weird."

"It's Lovers' Lake," they said at the same time.

"And?"

"I was an un-kissed sixteen-year-old boy looking for a little love," Jeff said, placing his hand over his heart dramatically. "Where better to look—"

"Than Lovers' Lake," I finished, "got it." I turned to Brett. "What about you? Were you looking for love at Lovers' Lake?"

Brett held up our joined hands. "Not anymore." Jeff made a vomiting noise and stood up, declared he was going to get a drink. "For the record," Brett whispered, too close again; my nerve endings were on high alert, "I was not an un-kissed sixteen-year-old boy."

"Let the world know," I called out, "Brett Wells was *not*

an un-kissed sixteen-year-old boy!" Brett laughed, pinching my lips. When he let go, I said, "If Jeff's your best friend, why doesn't he know the truth about us?"

"We don't really talk about that stuff."

"Right. Guys only talk about dirt and cars and whatever else is 'manly.' I forgot."

"That's not what I meant. Believe me, not telling Jeff is for the greater good."

"How so?" I asked.

Brett gave me a face, said, "Watch and learn," and called Jeff back over. I watched him run through the water, spraying a group of girls who shrieked, and sit back down next to Brett.

"What's up?"

"Duuuude," Brett said in this voice that did not sound like his, "did you see who went into the trees together?"

Jeff's eyes bulged out. "No. Who?"

"Tallani and Ryan." Brett nodded toward our left. "Just walked right through there. We saw the whole thing."

"No damn way! I thought they broke up!"

Brett looked at me and winked. To Jeff, he said, "Guess not."

Jeff, about to explode, ran away, re-splashing the same group of girls, who screamed even louder now.

"What was that about?" I asked.

"Give it a few minutes."

We sat and waited. At first, nothing. People were milling around, minding their business. Then there was a shift. People were whispering, leaning in closer. It was kind of amazing. And slowly, I started to realize exactly what Brett had done. A guy walked up to us, shaved head, white T-shirt, and bumped his fist against Brett's shoulder. "Did you hear about Tallani and Ryan?" he said, wiggling his eyebrows. "Explains why he's been missing so much practice."

I was dumbfounded.

Jeff actually could not be trusted.

Brett turned to me and brushed his shoulder in that stupid, prideful way. "See why I didn't tell Jeff?"

I mean, it was a good display. But there was one flaw. "You realize you just started a rumor about two people that's a complete lie, right?"

Brett began to say something. Shut his mouth. "Well—" Shut it again. Drew his eyebrows together. Then bit down on his lips, nodding. "I probably shouldn't have done that."

"Bingo."

"I was trying to make this a little more interesting. You don't seem too impressed by Lovers' Lake."

"Not at all."

"What does it take to impress you, Becca? A library? Maybe a bookstore?"

118

I bumped my knee against his. "I'll have you know I'm a multidimensional person, Brett. I do more than just read and study for calc."

"Yeah?" he asked, grin stretching impossibly wider.

The way he was looking at me made me nervous.

"Yeah." My voice was shaking. *Stop shaking!*

"Then why don't you show me one of those dimensions of yours," he said.

I wanted to catch him off guard, show Brett that there was more to me than the girl who kept her nose in a book. So, without thinking about it too much—and definitely without making a pro-con list—I leaned in and kissed him. It was quick. Maybe a second or two. Our lips barely touched. But it was nothing like that kiss in the hallway when we were strangers. Now my heart started to race and my fingers had a life of their own, wanting to latch onto his face and tug him closer. But I didn't do any of that.

I reminded myself this was fake and I pulled away.

I reminded myself that feelings, especially the weird ones stirring inside me right now, were dangerous. So I pushed them down, closed all the windows, and shut them out. I twisted the key to the lock on my heart and swallowed it whole. No one was getting in. Nothing was getting out.

I opened my eyes. His face was so close. I could see

the exact spot where the blue of his eyes was swallowed by his pupil. And he looked kind of stunned. Also a little impressed. I noticed how his navy long-sleeve shirt made his eyes look more blue. Even in the moonlight, they were *so damn blue*. And oh my god, what was happening to me tonight? Something was in the air at Lovers' Lake, because my heart had taken control of my brain.

This is fake, I reminded myself. And it was safer like that.

"What was that for?" Brett asked.

"For show," I said, all cool and casual.

Then he was smiling again. We were back on track.

The couple sitting in front of us stood up and disappeared into the trees. Brett nudged me, wiggled his eyebrows, and made these very weird noises. It was dumb. I laughed anyway. Then I realized that, aside from his football games, this was kind of my first time doing something normal. Like, high school normal. I hadn't gone to a party before. And it was all because of Brett. It was like he was slowly showing me that there was actually more to school than sitting in a class and taking notes. Which used to be all I wanted. But now, I was kind of wondering, had I been missing out all these years?

Brett stood up suddenly, said, "C'mon. We should get out before the rumor reaches Tallani or Ryan," and bent over again. I jumped onto his back and we were off, moving through the sloshy grass. People were watching us tonight, and it was the first time I really felt like we were a couple. I mean, holding hands in the hall was one thing. But tonight it actually *felt* like we were dating. And even if it was fake, it was still fun.

I was thinking that Brett must have been here before because his feet knew exactly where to go when he stopped in front of the lake. I sucked in a breath. Wow. It was beautiful. It almost made up for the gross walk over. From here, you could see where the two lakes met in the middle. There was still a sliver of land between them, like two halves of a heart that couldn't meet quite yet. And the moon was directly over the lake, making a small patch of water turn silver.

I went to jump off Brett's back, but his grip on my legs tightened.

"Brett?" I was whispering, like if I spoke too loud then it would ruin the peacefulness.

"Yeah?"

"What are you thinking about?"

"Jelly bells," he said.

I smacked my foot against his thigh. "Be serious."

"I am. Doesn't the moon kind of look like one?"

Then I was laughing really hard because he was right, it totally did.

Brett's hands loosened around my knees, and I hopped off his back. The ground was solid around this side of the lake. You could barely hear the people back at the party. Their voices were just a slight murmur.

"I get the appeal now," I said. "This is so pretty."

"Makes you want to sneak off into the trees, huh?"

I snorted. "Not *that* pretty."

Brett bumped his shoulder against mine.

I bumped his back.

"Sometimes," he said, "I forget places like this exist in Crestmont. Like I'm so focused on wanting to leave after high school that I forget there are reasons to stay."

"What do you want to do after we graduate?" I asked, realizing I didn't know.

Brett was staring intently at the water. "I don't know. Play football? I'm waiting to see what colleges are interested. I'm hoping to move somewhere big, like Atlanta. I want to be in a town that has more than a few thousand people."

"What about your family?"

"I think my parents want that future for me more than I do." Right. His dad's football dream. "What do you want to do?" He turned away from the lake now, watching me instead. I shifted from foot to foot, not knowing what to say.

"College is hard. I don't think my mom has the money to pay for it."

"You're smart," Brett said, "you can get a good scholarship."

"Maybe. Maybe not. I might have to stay here, help out at the bakery for a while and save up some money. College can wait."

"Yeah. Sometimes I wish the future could too."

We were quiet then. There were crickets chirping and the sound of water lapping against the shore. It was so much better here than back in the clearing. Then a weird noise came from the trees, a rustle, and I latched onto Brett's arm. "Did you hear that?" I whispered.

Brett took out his phone, turned on the flashlight, and pointed it in the direction the sound came from. "Hello?" he called.

The noise came again. This time it wasn't a rustle. It was more of a—

Moan.

The light exposed a couple hiding in the trees. The girl yelled, reaching up to cover her chest. I looked away, feeling the secondhand embarrassment. Brett fumbled with the flashlight, pointing it in my face while trying to shut it off. "Sorry!" he called out, walking backward. "We'll leave now. Uh, carry on."

We ran back through the forest, laughing so hard we had to stop to catch our breath.

My curfew was in an hour, but Brett had no intention of allowing the night to end with us catching two people going at it in the woods. So we hopped in his car and drove two towns over, which sounds far, but it barely took fifteen minutes. Why two towns? Brett wanted fast food. Apparently the only "respectable" burger, shake, and fries in all of Georgia were at Paul's Diner.

There was no Paul's Diner in Crestmont.

When our order was ready, we sat in Brett's car with the windows down, munching away on junk food at midnight. In five minutes I watched him inhale a burger, chocolate milk shake, and a large fry. It was equally impressive and gross. Now he was stealing *my* fries and dipping them into *my* strawberry shake and I was kind of annoyed but not really. The night was going well, so I was rolling with it.

"How do you know about this place?" I asked, slurping my shake. I was learning so much about Georgia tonight. And a little more about Brett.

He pointed down the road. "There's a park a few miles down. This huge stretch of grass with soccer fields and stuff. My dad and I used to come here when I was a kid on the weekends. This was before his promotion, back when he was home more often. We'd throw a football around for a few hours, then drive here for lunch. It was this tradition we had."

"My dad used to take me for ice cream after class," I said. "That was our thing."

Brett dipped his fry in my shake, held it out for me. "Is this our thing, then?" he asked. "Eating fast food at midnight in my car?"

I opened my mouth. He stuck the fry in. "I am totally okay with that."

"Me too."

"Why does your dad travel so much?" I knew his family had money, but I had no idea why.

"Have you seen that new hotel being built off the interstate?" I had. It was right when you drove into Crestmont, a few miles after the welcome sign. It was supposed to have its grand opening at the end of the month. "There's a bunch of them throughout the country, but this is the first one being built here. My dad works for them. He's the chief financial officer, does all that money stuff. So he flies around the country and checks in on different locations. Makes sure everything's running smoothly, I guess."

"What about your mom?"

"She doesn't work."

I wondered what that was like, to have enough money

to feel secure. Not having to worry about the price of tuition, student loans, or how much textbooks were going to cost. Having the ability to go to whatever school you wanted to.

"My mom always worked. She used to be a nurse," I said. "When she first opened the bakery, she was worried. It wasn't doing that well. Only a few customers per day. She invested so much money into it and I don't know what we would have done if it failed. A few months later, it started to take off. People were talking about it in town and we started getting huge orders. That's when I began helping out there. I don't think my mom expected the bakery to become so popular; she only hired, like, three people."

"I'm happy her business took off," Brett said. "I don't know what I'd do without jelly bells."

I smiled at him. "Me either."

"You know what would make this moment even better?"

"Jelly bells?"

"That too, yeah, but I was gonna say another burger. I'll be right back."

How was he still hungry? And how did he stay in such good shape? There must have been some secret gym routine he was on, plus the intense football training.

I was watching Brett outside the car; he was rummaging through his pockets, probably looking for his wallet, when a car pulled into the spot in front of us. I was expecting more teenagers craving something greasy like us. Instead it was an older couple holding hands, and wow, that car looked expensive. Like, way too expensive for this town. Brett must've noticed them too because he was hovering outside, watching. I thought he was admiring their ride because he was standing there, frozen. One of his hands was still on the door handle. Did all guys have a thing for nice cars?

But then I really looked at his face. His mouth was wide open and he looked like he'd just been punched in the gut.

He jumped back inside, mumbled something about having to leave, and sped out of the parking lot. I barely had time to put my seat belt on and went flying into the door when he turned onto the road. "Slow down!" I yelled, placing the cup between my thighs so it wouldn't spill. "Brett!"

He was driving so fast. I looked at him and it was like he was in a different world. His eyes were locked on the road; his hands had a death grip on the wheel. His lips were moving. Was he talking to himself? He looked like he was either going to cry or hit something.

"Brett, you're scaring me. Slow down." He was mumbling so low I turned the radio off to hear him. "What?"

"I have to get out of here," he said.

"Brett." I reached out, placed my hand on his arm. "Pull over."

"He's not supposed to be here."

"Who? What are you talking about?"

I watched the needle on the speedometer go higher. Higher. Higher. Until it was nearly at one hundred. We were going to crash and die and my body would be covered in a strawberry milk shake when the police found us.

"Brett." I leaned across the middle, placed my hand directly over his on the wheel. "You need to slow down."

Brett blinked, shook his head, then glanced down at my hand on his. He looked at me, must've seen the terrified look on my face, and swore under his breath. Then we were slowing down. Finally, Brett pulled over, shut the engine off, and buried his head in his hands.

I was speechless.

I breathed in. Out. In. Out. Did a mental count of my body parts. Wiggled my toes. Wiggled my fingers. Ten each. I told myself we were both okay. When I was sure I could speak, I said, "What was that?"

No response.

"Brett?"

Nothing.

"You're freaking me out. Did you know those people?" It was too dark for me to see their faces clearly, but they didn't look like anyone I knew. And Crestmont was pretty small, so I'd probably recognize them at least.

Then I remembered that no, we weren't in Crestmont anymore. So how did Brett know them?

He lifted his head off the wheel and rested it back against the seat. His eyes were closed, his chest moving in and out too quickly. Was he having a panic attack? Should I call an ambulance? When I took my phone out, he placed his hand on top of mine. "I'm fine," he said, sounding anything but.

"What was that?"

"I don't know."

"*Who* was that?" I tried instead.

"I don't want to know."

This was making less and less sense by the second.

Then my heart dropped, plummeted right into my stomach, because Brett said, "I think that was my dad. And that woman wasn't my mom."

Oh.

Oh.

"But I— You said your dad was in Ohio." As soon as I said it, I realized how dumb it was. And then everything sort of clicked into place, a puzzle neither of us wanted to solve.

"I thought he was," Brett whispered.

I reached for him—his hand, his arm, anything. I latched on. Tight. I knew what it felt like to drown without water. It was worse when no one was there to bring you back to shore.

I held his hand. Squeezed it really tight.

"Are you sure that was him?" I asked because it was dark out and I was desperate for this look to leave Brett's face.

Brett didn't say anything. We sat there, parked on the side of the road while cars rushed by. I didn't know what to say. Hell, I'd been through this too. Well, a different version, but it was still the same. And if that really was his dad, I knew there were no words to help. No "sorry" could fix this wound.

"Do you have a book?" Brett asked.

What? "Um. Yeah. Somewhere in here." I pulled my bag onto my lap, rummaged through it.

"I need a distraction."

Right. That made sense. Mom's baking. My reading. They were both distractions.

"Do you have it?" he asked again, sounding panicked.

I pulled out the book. Brett sighed, undid his seat belt, and reclined his chair back. He wrapped his arms around himself and closed his eyes. He looked so different than he had earlier. Smaller. Sadder.

"Are you okay?" I whispered, wanting to reach out and hold him.

"Read to me" was all he said.

"I don't think you'll like this book." It was romantic. Like, embarrassingly so.

"Please, Becca."

I flipped open to the page I had bookmarked and began to read. My voice sounded weird at first, more high-pitched, but then it evened out and I started to sound like me again.

Reading out loud was weird. I was so used to occupying this fictional world alone that having Brett there with me felt different. Not a bad different. Just different. I wasn't sure if he was even listening. He kind of looked like he was sleeping. I kept pausing after each paragraph, sneaking a peek at him.

After I finished the first chapter, our eyes met. He said, "Keep going."

So I kept reading.

That was the first time I missed curfew.

Brett

HE WASN'T IN OHIO.

That was his car. His suit. Those were his hands holding someone else's.

That was my dad.

But it wasn't my mom.

It didn't make any sense, because my dad would never . . .

I couldn't even think the word. It all felt wrong. A never-ending nightmare.

He was supposed to be on a business trip. In Ohio. At a hotel. He was supposed to be in meetings and talking to staff and dealing with financial stuff. He wasn't supposed to be at diners in the middle of the night with a woman I'd never seen before. And he was not supposed to be holding her hand like that.

Like Becca had said, it was dark. And even though I knew it was my dad, there was this voice in my head that kept saying *but what if it wasn't?* I clung to that voice because it was easier to be confused than to be angry. With confusion there were still possibilities; it wasn't black and white just yet. And there was a shred of hope somewhere in the gray that I needed right now.

It was better than the opposite: convincing myself it really was my dad. What would that mean? Were all those business trips a lie? They couldn't be. He brought back souvenirs from each state. But what else was he doing while he was away? What was he doing when he wasn't working?

Then I remembered when he came home from New York last weekend and didn't bring me anything. Was he even in New York? Probably not. He was here the whole time. Wasn't he?

But maybe it wasn't him.

It was, though.

It was him.

The next morning my head felt like it had been put in a blender. I woke up to a text from my mom. She was at yoga, then going for lunch. She wouldn't be home for a few hours.

Then it hit me like a ton of bricks. *My mom.* My mom, who was in love with my dad. My mom, who had spent nearly twenty years of her life with him. I realized that this wasn't just about me. This could ruin her too.

I decided then that I couldn't tell her what I had seen. Not until I knew for sure.

I needed answers.

I took a shower and called Becca. She picked up right away, probably still worried about me. I remembered her voice in the darkness last night, reading to me. I needed that again right now. That small sense of peace. That certainty.

"Can you come over?" I asked.

A half hour later my doorbell rang. Becca was standing on the porch, hunched over. "Hi," she said, out of breath.

"Becca—did you run here?"

She stepped inside, chest heaving. "Y-Yeah. It sounded urgent. Didn't have a ride. You good?"

I stared at her: hair sticking to her forehead, bent over like she was about to pass out, mouth hanging open as she tried to catch her breath. This girl had literally run across town to my house. She looked like she needed an ambulance, yet the only thing she seemed to be worrying about was me. I hugged her, wrapped her into my chest until my chin was resting on the top of her head. I felt it then, the same feeling as last night, when she was reading to me. That stillness. A break in the storm.

"Thank you," I said.

I let go. She fixed her hair, cheeks flushed. "Yeah. Of course. What's up?" I led her to the kitchen. She kept glancing around. I thought she was admiring the house at first—my mom went overboard with the decorating—but then I saw her peeking through doorways and trying to look upstairs.

"No one's home," I told her.

She visibly relaxed.

We took a seat at the kitchen table. I got her two water bottles, just in case. "I need your help," I said when she'd nearly finished the first.

"Does this have to do with your dad?"

I nodded. "Read any books about detectives?"

Turned out that yeah, she had.

We started in his office. It felt weird being in there—my dad was pretty strict on no one going inside. I looked around the room. Everything was organized. The books in the shelves were in alphabetical order; the papers on the desk were stacked in neat-edged piles. Everything looked polished and shiny. Becca went right to his computer, saying something about checking his credit card history. "The computer has a password," she said, staring at the screen with her eyes narrowed. "Any ideas?"

She was going all Nancy Drew. I was kind of into it.

I walked over and stood beside her. "Try my name." She typed it in. The password box shook and turned red. It was wrong. "Try Willa, my mom's name." Again, no luck. We tried birthdays, anniversaries, names of pets my parents used to have—nothing worked.

It was a dead end.

"What now?" I asked.

Becca rubbed her hands together, placed her chin on top. She was thinking hard, chewing on her lips. I realized she did that a lot when she was deep in thought. Even sometimes when she read.

I was staring at her mouth, kind of mesmerized, when she said, "We need to check something that's not on his computer. Do you know what time his flight left yesterday? Brett?"

I cleared my throat. "Ten thirty." She typed something into her phone. "Hey, let me see," I said, crouching to peer over her shoulder. She was on the airport's website, checking the flight records for anything out of Atlanta, Georgia, to Columbus, Ohio. She kept tapping. Every time the screen reloaded, my chest constricted. I couldn't look anymore. I walked to the other side of the room and sat on the couch, fingers crossed.

All I needed was a little hope. Some good news.

"Found it!" Becca ran to the couch and showed me the screen. There was a flight to Columbus out of Atlanta and it left yesterday morning. At ten thirty.

It felt like my heart had just been connected to a defibrillator and given a shock. It was beating again.

"That's a good sign," Becca said. "Maybe he really is in Ohio and that man you saw last night was . . . someone else."

"You really believe that?" I asked her.

She said yes, but the look on her face said otherwise.

"You're not a very good liar, Becca."

She sighed. "I'm sorry. I'm trying to stay hopeful. Do you know what hotel he's staying at? We can call and see if he checked in."

That was a good idea. My dad usually stayed at the United Suites, the hotel company he worked for, but I texted my mom to make sure. When she typed back that same hotel, I looked up the phone number—luckily, there was only one in Columbus—and Becca made the call.

The phone was ringing. My hands were trembling. I couldn't stop bouncing my foot against the floor.

"Hi," Becca said. I almost fell off the couch. "I was

wondering if you can see if a guest checked in yesterday afternoon? The name is—" She looked at me, eyebrows raised.

"Thomas," I mouthed.

"Thomas Wells," she finished. "Yeah, he's my, uh, dad. He hasn't been answering his phone and we're worried." Becca was nodding along to whatever the receptionist said. I leaned in closer, trying to hear. "It's Thomas. Yeah, W-E-L-L-S. Sure. I'm on hold," she whispered. A second later, she said, "Oh. Okay. Thanks anyway. Bye."

She hung up.

"Well?"

I didn't like the look on her face.

"She said there was no reservation under that name."

It felt like the floor had turned to quicksand and I was being sucked under.

"Brett—" She reached for me. I walked away. Down the hall and up the stairs until I was in my parents' room. I searched through the closet. Checked inside all his jacket pockets. Then the dresser drawers, the nightstands. There was nothing there. No shady restaurant receipts. No perfume that smelled nothing like my mom's. Jesus Christ. It was dead end after dead end.

I was sitting on the floor when I heard the door creak open. Becca walked in, looking a little uncomfortable. I think I may have been crying, because I was sort of seeing two of her instead of one.

"You know," she said, kneeling on the floor beside me and sitting down, "when my parents got divorced, I felt like this too. I kept searching for answers like their marriage was some puzzle and all I needed was to find the right pieces. I obsessed over it for years, wondering why my dad left and what moment he realized he didn't want us anymore. Was it during dinner one night? Was there a fight I don't know about? Did he just stop loving my mom? There are so many questions and I'm still looking for the answers, Brett. Even now. I mean"—she started laughing—"I show up at his house sometimes and I just stand there like a complete weirdo! Staring and waiting! I even went *inside* last week and talked to his wife! And the worst part is, I don't even know what I'm waiting for. I just stand there and hope that the day will come when I won't have to. When I won't feel like this anymore.

"And some days are better. Like when we were at the arcade eating jelly bells. Or when I'm at the bakery with my mom and Cassie. In those moments, it's like the life we used to have with my dad was from another lifetime. And I'm happy with it being just my mom and me. But there are days when it sucks. Days when I obsess over him and overanalyze every little thing until I realize it's pointless. People leave,

Brett. It's not our fault for not giving them a reason to stay. It's their fault for not finding one. You know?"

No. I didn't know. Because up until this moment my life had been contained in this perfect little bubble: perfect house, perfect football career, perfect family—everything was so damn perfect. Too perfect. And now there were dents. Cracks. And I kept thinking back to the way my mom looked during dinner when she dropped that glass of wine. And the night when I found her in her bedroom crying after my dad left for New York. Or the morning he came back and she stood there on the porch, not saying a word. And I felt like a complete idiot for not realizing that being perfect was just a facade. An act. That if you pulled back the curtain, there was a whole lot of shit hiding behind it.

"My dad's having an affair." I whispered the words, like maybe if I said it low enough it would make it less true.

"Yeah," Becca said. Her hand slid across the floor and grabbed on to mine. "He is."

Becca

WHEN IN DOUBT, RETURN TO the trusty pro-con list.

I made myself at home in Brett's bedroom. Which is probably one of the weirder places I've been this year. Weeks ago, if someone told me I'd be spending my Saturday afternoon sitting on Brett Wells's bed, I would have laughed in their face.

Once Brett dug out a notebook and pen from his desk drawer, I went to town. I drew a line down the center of the page and wrote PROS on one side and CONS on the other. The list was to decide whether or not it was a good idea to tell his mom about his dad's affair. Or, on a heavier note, possible *multiple* affairs.

Brett was sitting at his desk chair, his head still in his hands. It was physically painful for me to see him like this and not know what to do to help him. I of all people should know some magical word to ease the pain at least momentarily. But nope. I had nothing. Nada. His world was falling apart and the only solution my brain could conjure up was a dumb list.

It was quite literally all we had. The pressure was on.

I tapped the pen against my knee, thinking out loud. "A con could be that there's always the slim chance it wasn't your dad we saw." Brett made a noise, almost a snort, and didn't look up. "Maybe telling your mom will do more harm than good. Like she'd prefer to not know instead of everything changing with the truth. Ignorance is bliss and all that."

"That would make two of us," Brett mumbled.

I filled in the CON side of the list with the two bullets.

"Pro would be that you don't have to keep a secret from your mom and that she deserves to know the truth. I'd want to know if it were me."

Brett stood up. "This is ridiculous, Becca. We're seriously using a list to figure out whether we should break my mom's heart?"

I gripped the notebook a little tighter. "They help me make decisions."

"But it's not helping me," he said, storming out of the room.

I hated this. Feeling like there was nothing I could say or do that would make this easier on him. But there had to be *something*. This wasn't some book I was reading, where the future was already planned out. I still had a chance to change Brett's story. So what was I going to do?

I had an idea. It was there, in the back of my mind. I kept thinking about last night, when Brett said he wanted to be distracted, that it would help him process. And I had the perfect distraction. But it was personal. Like, very personal. And it was one of the things I wrote on my own pro-con list about dating Brett—the one con that scared me the most.

I tried to put everything into perspective. Brett was going through a lot right now, and I knew exactly what having your world turned upside down felt like. And I wished I would have let someone help me through it instead of bottling all my emotions up. Maybe then I'd be better now, more in the present instead of stuck in the past. That was five years ago. I couldn't go back and rewrite my own story. But Brett's was happening right now. And if there was a slim chance I could help him, even for one night, wasn't it worth it?

I crossed the list out on the page. Then I put the notebook down on the desk and followed Brett downstairs.

I found him sitting on the couch, staring up at the ceiling. "Hey," I said, sitting beside him. He hadn't smiled all day.

Brett brushed his fingers against mine. "Sorry for getting mad," he said. "This is a lot. It's like everything I thought about my life, my parents, their marriage, was all a lie. I want to call my dad right now and ask him. I want answers. But the thought of having them is terrifying, Becca. What am I supposed to do?"

His eyes were red, staring into mine. I realized he'd run out of the room to cry.

"The thing is," I said, "you don't have to do anything right now. I know it seems like life or death, but all of this weight will still be there tomorrow, Brett. You can make a decision then. Tonight, you should come to my house for dinner." I paused. Forced the words out. "With me and my mom."

"I thought you didn't want your mom to know about us?"

"I don't. I really don't. But you need a change of scenery right now. Being in this house is not helping you."

"You'd really do that for me?" he asked. It made me sad that he sounded surprised.

"Of course." How bad could Brett fiasco number two really be?

Brett rested his head against mine, exhaling a long breath.

"You're the best girlfriend I never had, Becca Hart."

Saying I was nervous for this dinner would be an understatement. I was visibly freaking out. My feet were tapping against the elevator floor, and I swear this thing was moving faster than normal because suddenly the doors were opening and we were standing in front of my apartment.

"Remember," I whispered to Brett, "no talking about fake anything. Got it?"

He still wasn't giving me that ultra-Brett smile, but his lips twitched a little. It was a start.

"Got it."

With my heart somewhere in my stomach, I knocked.

"Don't you have keys to your house?" Brett asked.

Of course I had keys to my house. I was just too nervous to remember. Dammit. I grabbed them from my pocket and had the key in the lock as soon as the door pulled open. My mom looked at me, then Brett, then back to me about a thousand times. I swear it happened in slow motion. Every agonizing second ticked by and I saw the exact moment the realization hit her.

"This is a surprise," she said, tucking her hair behind her ears.

"Mom," I said, giving her the please-do-not-embarrass-me look, "you remember Brett. My"—*c'mon, Becca. Spit it out*—"boyfriend."

She gasped, hand flying over her mouth and everything. One second in and the regret was oh so present.

"Brett! From the bakery! You're the one who made Bells drop all of the cannoli—"

"Thanks for bringing that up, Mom."

"—of course I remember you, dear. Come on in."

"It's nice to meet you, Ms. Hart," Brett said, kind as ever. Then he gave her The Smile. She was a goner.

Good god, mother. And I thought I was the one who had to keep it together.

"You can call me Amy, hon. I wish Becca would have told me we were having a guest for dinner," my mom said, casting me a not-so-subtle glare. "I would have made something fancier than hamburgers."

"Hamburgers are fine, Mom. That's his favorite anyway."

"They are?" she asked, gesturing for the two of us to step inside.

"Yeah." Brett turned to me, eyebrows drawn together. "I didn't think you remembered that."

I shrugged, moved my hair in front of my shoulders to block my stupid cheeks, which felt as hot as the sun. Thankfully, my mom led us into the kitchen then and the attention was taken off my ability to memorize random facts about Brett. The air smelled like grease and meat instead of its usual warm vanilla scent. My mom ran to the stove and was juggling two trays in her hands. "Have a seat, you two. It'll just be another minute."

I sat down while Brett walked to my mom's side and shut the door to the oven. Total butt kisser. She was eyeing him like she was trying to visually measure what size tux he'd wear for our wedding. I hoped Brett didn't notice. Or see the thumbs-up she gave me when he had his back turned.

This was going to be a long night.

When we were all seated and my mom seemed to get over her initial shock, she said, "So, when did this happen? Becca kept telling me that you two were only friends."

"A few weeks ago," Brett said.

I coughed. Really, really loud.

Brett stopped pilling fries on his plate to give me a confused look.

"What Brett means," I said, doing damage control, "is that we've been talking for a few weeks, as *friends*, and we just recently started dating. Right, Brett?"

"Yes. Exactly." Then he shoved a handful of fries in his mouth. Good. Now he couldn't talk and mess all this up.

Thankfully my mom had her love blinders on and didn't notice the slipup. She was grinning at the two of us like a weirdo. And for once I was thankful Brett ate so damn fast. At least this dinner would be over soon.

* * *

The tour I gave Brett of our apartment ended in my bedroom. It was funny: I started the day off in his bedroom and now we were in mine.

And by funny I meant severely nerve-racking.

His eyes instantly locked on the wall that was floor-to-ceiling bookshelves. I had it color coordinated. I was very proud.

"You've read all of these?" he asked.

"Most more than once," I said.

I sat on the middle of my bed and folded my hands in my lap. I felt very awkward. Not in an uncomfortable way. More in a this-is-the-first-time-a-boy-has-been-in-my-room kind of way. The butterflies were back, flapping away in my stomach.

Brett's gaze went from the books to the posters covering my yellow walls. They were mostly bands I listened to when I was younger or posters from some of my favorite books that had been made into movies. For the record, the book was always better.

"Your room is nice," he said, sitting on the edge of my bed. "Exactly what I was expecting."

"And by that you mean you were expecting to see a lot of books."

"Pretty much. Yeah." Brett laughed and I gasped, pointing my finger at him.

"You laughed!"

"So?"

"You haven't laughed all day. I've been waiting for it."

He watched me for a moment with a crease between his brows before turning to the photo on my nightstand. It was my mom and me hugging. It was so sunny outside that day that you could barely even see our faces with the glare.

Brett picked up the photo. "When's this from?" he asked.

"My thirteenth birthday party. That was back when my mom was a horrible cook. She made my birthday cake that year with salt instead of sugar. It was disgusting. No one ate it. We took that picture right before the sun set."

"Was that your favorite birthday?"

"No," I said. "It was the first one without my dad." I grabbed the frame from his hands and gently placed it back on the nightstand.

Brett scooted across the bed, moving a little closer until his back was against the headboard. "You were right about getting out of my house. Being here with you and your mom worked. I feel better. It kind of makes everything else shrink a little bit."

"You can come over whenever," I said. "I know my mom would love that. You could move in if you want. She'd probably be fine with me having a roommate."

He laughed again. "She's a little overenthusiastic, huh?"

"She just wants me to be happy. I think, after the divorce, she was worried it had ruined me or something. That I'd turn into this emotionless robot that doesn't believe in love and spends the rest of her life alone with a few dozen cats."

"But you don't believe in love."

No. *But I'm starting to believe in* like.

Shut up, brain.

"I believe in love," I said, "I just don't think it's worth the risk. Like when you're dating someone, you're either going to end up marrying that person or having your heart broken. It's a fifty-fifty chance. And even if you do marry them, there's *another* fifty percent chance you'll end up divorced. At what point do people realize the odds are always stacked against them?"

"Isn't that what makes it so special when you find the right person? The fact that you two were able to beat the odds?"

"Sure, but there's still so many downsides to falling in love. Reading, however," I said, pointing toward my glorious bookshelf, "gives you all the fun without the pain. A great alternative."

"I may have to borrow a book or two if my parents' marriage goes to shit."

I hit him with my elbow. "Don't say that, Brett. You don't know what's going to happen." I mean, I kind of did know what was going to happen, based on my parents' track record and simple statistics. But I was holding out hope for Brett's sake. He deserved that.

"I can make a pretty good guess," he said.

This distraction technique was not working.

"You know what?" I hopped out of bed and grabbed my laptop, tossing it to him. "I'll be right back." I ran to the kitchen and grabbed a tub of cotton candy ice cream from the freezer, assured my mom we'd leave the door open (cue eye roll), then raced back to my room before she could say anything else equally mortifying.

Brett took one look at the ice cream and said, "Don't tell me you actually like that crap."

"Cotton candy ice cream?" I asked, completely appalled. "It's my favorite."

I made a big show of opening the container and scooping out a huge spoonful, then ate the entire thing. I even licked the spoon for good measure.

Brett looked like he was trying not to gag.

"Got any jelly bells?" he asked.

"Nope."

Ignoring his horrible ice cream taste, I sat back down on the bed and opened my laptop to Netflix. "I realized," I said, "that everyone thinks we're dating and we haven't even gone on our first date yet. That's not acceptable."

"Completely unacceptable," Brett agreed.

"So it only makes sense—"

"Only makes sense."

"—if we declare this as our first official date. And stop mocking me. What movie do you want to watch?" I scrolled through all the different genres.

"Something scary," he said quickly. Suspiciously quick.

"You should know I love scary movies," I said. "So if you're expecting me to get all cuddly, it's not going to happen."

Brett pouted. I chose the movie. It was about a family who moved out of their haunted house only to move into a new house that was also haunted. Really unique, ground-breaking stuff.

I ate my way through the entire ice cream carton within the first half hour. I choked on it a few times from laughing so hard. The movie wasn't funny. It was Brett. He was jumping and shrieking at every little thing. He even covered his face with a pillow at one point.

To make it worse, I held out a spoonful of ice cream to his face. "Want some?"

He pushed it away, pretending to throw up.

A few seconds later he mumbled, "I can't believe I have a crush on a girl with such horrible ice cream taste."

My whole body tensed. I was warm all over. I could feel my heart trying to burst free from the cage I had it locked in. And for a single, tiny second, I considered it. I glanced at Brett. He was staring at the screen way too intensely. Okay. So I guess we were both pretending he never said that. Plus, this whole thing was fake. So he was just acting. There was no way he meant that . . .

I hid my smile behind the spoon.

When I woke up the next morning, Brett was still lying in bed beside me. We must have fallen asleep during the movie. I sat up quickly, tensing when I heard the *thump!* of my laptop falling off my bed. Then I noticed the plate at the foot of the bed with jelly bells on it. There were two pieces of paper tucked underneath. One had *Becca* scrawled on it in my mom's signature cursive. The other read *Brett*.

Brett

MY DAD'S FIRST BUSINESS TRIP happened last year. He got another promotion at work and took our family out for dinner a town over to celebrate. The restaurant was Italian, really fancy. It had bottles of wine waiting on the table and dim lighting. Even the menu felt expensive. Everything was over thirty dollars and written in Italian. My mom never stopped smiling. I was happy too because they were happy and we were all together.

In the middle of the meal my dad broke the news. He said with his promotion came more responsibility. That he'd have to travel through the country to advise on different hotel locations. He said the company was relying on him and he had to impress them. He said he couldn't say no.

My mom looked thrilled. Just another thing to add to our family's accomplishments. I was sad; it felt like my heart had dropped. I didn't want my dad to leave for weeks. I didn't even want him gone for a few days. But what was I supposed to do when they both looked so happy? Beaming at me and waiting for a reaction? So I told my dad that yeah, that was fine. That I was happy. That being able to travel the country for work sounded cool. He told me that someday I'd travel too, for football.

My mom ordered another bottle of wine and my dad carried her into the house when we got home. He left for his first trip the next weekend. It was in Buffalo, New York. A new hotel had opened right near the border with Ontario for travelers coming across. My dad packed his bags and they were all lined up in a row near the front door. He had his briefcase and his new custom-tailored suit. The taxi came up the driveway and my mom kissed him goodbye. She said she loved him and he said it back. And it looked like they meant it. It really did. I could see it in her eyes and the way he held her face in his hands. It was real.

My dad patted my shoulder and told me to watch over my mom while he was gone. Then he left, got into the taxi and headed off to the airport.

That first weekend without him was better than I thought it would be. Jeff and other guys from the team came over and we ordered pizza. We watched recordings of our last football game. Coach wanted us to study them, see where we went wrong and where we could improve. And my mom seemed okay, lingering around and checking in on us. My dad was gone, but we were fine. Sure, I missed him, but it was hard to miss someone too much when you knew they'd be coming home in two days.

When my dad came back, he brought me a new gym bag and some stuff he'd gotten from the hotel with the logo on it. Water bottles, key chains—those sorts of things. My mom was thrilled. I was thrilled.

But now I couldn't stop thinking back to all those trips.

Over the past year, there had been dozens of them. And I kept trying to remember any sort of detail that would tell me when business trips stopped being business trips. Was there a day when my mom stopped seeming happy when he returned? Was there one trip where she didn't say "I love you" before he left? I was so excited by the gifts he brought me that I didn't even think to pause and check if they were actually from the state he was supposedly in.

I couldn't stop looking back. I wished the past had been recorded like my football games. Then I could rewatch it all, rewind to the moment everything changed.

Then I remembered what Becca said about searching for answers to a puzzle that could never be solved. That sounded like complete hell. I didn't want to look back five years from now and still not know the truth.

I had to know.

I decided to tell my mom.

I had the sinking suspicion she already knew. Looking back on the past few weeks, there were some signs. The crying. The way she seemed sad, quiet. Her spilling wine during dinner and my parents' hushed conversations behind closed doors. It was all adding up, these little clues I was too busy to pay attention to before. But now they were there, impossible to ignore.

I hoped my mom didn't know. Because if she knew about my dad's lies all this time and decided to keep it from me, I wasn't sure how I'd react.

And if she had known all this time and was suffering through it alone? That would make me feel even worse.

Another part of me hoped that my mom would have some answers. Like when I told her about seeing my dad with another woman, she'd have a perfect explanation for all of this and my life would return to its normal routine of football games and fake relationships. Like maybe it was an old friend of his. Maybe it was my mom wearing a wig. Not that it would make any damn sense, but it was a lot easier to think about than the alternative.

I made the decision to tell her when I was driving home

from Becca's apartment the next morning. Spending the night watching her and her mom changed something in my head. It was like a little bit of reassurance that no matter what the truth ended up being, there was still a chance my family would be okay like hers was. It made me realize that I wasn't going through this alone either. I had my mom like Becca had hers.

I had Becca too.

Then there was that quietness between us after what I said last night, about having a crush on her. I wasn't sure why I said it aloud or what even made me say it. But then the words were out there in the universe and they felt right. I was starting to care about her. How could I not after what she'd done for me? Sticking by my side for all of this? Our relationship was supposed to be fake. We had a clear contract that began and ended at school. But she'd given me more than that. She'd given me her weekends and her weeknights. She'd let me into her home. The girl literally ran over to my house because I needed her. And the dinner with her mom—putting me before herself like that? How could you not like someone with a heart so big?

But I knew Becca's stance on love and relationships. Which was her exact reasoning for having a fake one. I didn't know what to do now. How to act without pushing her too far and scaring her away. I was walking a thin line in all aspects of my life. And with my parents' future dangling in front of me, like a string that was slowly beginning to fray, it felt way too selfish to even dig into my feelings for Becca right now.

I pulled into my driveway and my entire body tensed. My dad's car was parked right there. He was home. And hell, it felt so weird to feel nervous right now. My dad coming home used to be the highlight of my week and now I was here, hiding in my car because I was too scared to walk into my own house and face the truth.

How could one night at a diner change my life this much?

I walked inside. "Mom?" I called, looking around warily.

"Up here!" she yelled from upstairs. I followed her voice into her bedroom, where she was standing in front of a full-length mirror wearing a dress. There was a man pulling the fabric around her hips with a tape measure hanging from his mouth.

"Too tight?" he asked. I watched him stick a pin into the dress.

"That's great. Can we shorten the length a little? I don't want it to drag. Oh, hi, hon. Did you see your father when you came in? He's somewhere downstairs."

"No. What's going on?" I asked.

"This is Carlos. He's helping me with my dress for the hotel's grand opening this weekend."

"That's *this* weekend?"

"Yes, Brett. Didn't you see your father's text? We've been calling you all morning. And where were you last night?" Before I could even answer, she was moving on. "The hotel's opening this weekend and they're throwing a party to celebrate. Your father and I will be there, of course, and you will as well. Go grab your suit and try it on. If you need a new one, Carlos will need to get started quickly."

I didn't move. I felt like I'd been sucked into another dimension.

"Brett? Your suit."

They were both staring at me like I'd lost it.

"Can I talk to you for a second, Mom? Alone?"

"After you try on your suit."

Slightly dazed, I went to my room and put on the damn suit. I kept listening for the sound of my dad walking up the stairs but everything was drowned out by my mom yelling my name every two seconds. "Brett! Hurry up!"

"I'm coming!"

It felt completely fucked up to be talking about suits and hotels and parties and dress sizes when I had this huge secret that felt like it was going to claw its way out of my mouth any second.

When my mom saw me, she covered her mouth with her hands. "Oh, Brett. You look so handsome. Isn't he handsome? Come here. Let me see."

I stood there while they hovered around, poking and pulling. "Hey, Mom? Where's Dad?"

"Thomas!" she yelled, tugging at the fabric on my wrist. "Maybe in the basement. Do you have a tie to wear with this? You can borrow one of your father's."

It all felt so wrong.

"Mom." I said it firmer this time. "Can we talk for a second?"

Sensing that something was off, she stopped fixing my suit. Her eyes lifted to mine and she signaled for Carlos to give us a minute alone. "Something wrong?" she asked when it was just the two of us.

Now what? Where was I supposed to start? How did I even bring something like this up?

"Remember when Dad left for New York a few weeks ago?" I asked. My mom nodded, taking a seat on the bed. "I walked into your room that night and you were sleeping. You'd been crying, Mom. There were tissues everywhere." She was just staring at me, not saying a word. "Why were you so sad?"

A long moment dragged by. "You know it's always hard on me when your father leaves."

It felt like a scripted response from a book. *How to Pretend Like Everything is Okay.*

"Because you miss him?" I prodded.

"Of course I miss him when he's gone."

"But you weren't happy when he came home."

My mom tensed, looked down at her lap. Then she patted the bed beside her and I sat down. She grabbed my hands. Hers were cold. I stared at the wedding band on her finger.

I tried to remember the last time we'd talked like this and couldn't. I was always talking to my dad about football and college. My mom was always listening and smiling. That was the dynamic. And now I couldn't even read her face to see if something was off because I didn't know how to.

"I must have been preoccupied with something else, Brett. I'm always happy when your dad comes home. You know that."

"But you weren't happy. You just stood there. You didn't walk down the driveway to talk to him. Then that night during dinner you spilled wine everywhere. You started to cry, remember? Then you went up to your room and Dad followed. And I heard you guys talking—"

Her hand tightened around mine. The ring cut into my finger. "You heard us?"

"Well, no. The doors were closed. I couldn't hear much. What were you talking about?"

"Your dad and I talk about a lot of things. Many of them you don't need to worry about. I must have been having an off night. That's it." She smiled, pulling herself together. "There's nothing you need to worry about. Your father is home and the hotel is opening this weekend. This is a good thing, Brett. A happy time, okay? Don't worry about me and your father. Everything is fine."

No wonder I was good at pretending to be Becca's boyfriend. Apparently being a good actor was genetic.

Now I felt even more lost than I had when I walked in. There were no answers. At least not for now. Maybe I should have felt relieved that my life would stay the same for another few weeks. But that didn't really feel like enough anymore. That doubt was always going to be there in the back of my mind until someone gave me a reason not to be doubtful anymore.

"Mom," I said, "if something was wrong between you and Dad, you'd tell me, right?"

"We're fine, Brett."

"But would you tell me?"

She sighed. "Of course."

"And you'd want me to tell you?"

"What do you mean?"

"Like, if I thought something was off with Dad . . . you'd want to know?"

I could see it then, in her eyes. Because my mom was always gentle and soft-spoken. She never got angry or raised her voice. I couldn't even remember a time when she'd yelled at me. Maybe that's why it was so clear to me that she was upset.

"Brett." Her voice was low and she kept glancing at the door. "Did you—" The door to the bedroom opened and my dad walked in. My mom jumped and whatever she was going to say was long gone. She stood up too quickly and smiled at him. All traces of anger were gone. "There you are! Brett was just trying on his suit for the hotel's opening."

My parents turned to me, waiting.

"Yeah. It, uh, fits."

My dad dropped his luggage on the bed and pulled me in for a hug. I felt like I was suffocating. "How was your game?" he asked, releasing me.

"We won."

"And your girlfriend?"

It took me a second to remember he knew about Becca. My mom, however, did not.

"What about her?" I asked.

"I'm assuming she's coming this weekend," he said, unpacking his clothes. They were stacked perfectly in his luggage. It reminded me of the papers on his office desk. The snooping. The lies. "Your mother and I want to meet her."

I was torn between keeping Becca away from this mess and selfishly wanting her there. The entire reason I started this fake relationship was for this exact purpose, having my dad think I was dating. But now, spinning a lie to impress him seemed like a mistake. At least lying was something we had in common.

"She'll be there," I said, forcing a smile.

By the way my dad smiled back, he didn't suspect a thing.

Becca

THE WEEK FLEW BY. SUDDENLY my fake relationship with Brett was starting to feel more like two amateur detectives solving a mystery neither of them was qualified for. If I had known this was going to happen, I would have thrown a few mystery books into my weekly mix. Maybe then we'd have more to go on than an iffy parking lot spotting and a gut feeling.

It was Monday afternoon and we were walking through town. I had a stack of Hart's Cupcakes flyers between my arms. Brett was holding the tape and stapler. Mom was so proud to find out that the extra advertisements had worked (thanks, Jenny) that she had us sticking them up anywhere we could. Half the lampposts in Crestmont now had a pink sheet of paper stuck to them.

When we had none left, I suggested we reward ourselves for all this intensive labor. Naturally, we ended up back at the arcade. Brett was playing Whac-A-Mole. He was hitting them way too hard like he had a personal vendetta against fake moles. There was no way he wanted another stuffed whale *that* badly. He was also ranting about the hotel's grand opening this weekend and some guy named Carlos who was poking him with pins. I needed more context on that one.

"She was completely clueless," he was saying. Whack. "I dropped so many hints, Becca, and my mom just sat there like she had no idea what I was talking about." Another whack. "But she knows something. I know she does. I just don't know what she knows because she won't tell me that she knows it. So how am I supposed to tell her that I know what she knows?"

I blinked. "What?"

Another whack. The game ended and Brett ripped out the tickets, shoving them into his pocket. A few fell onto the floor and I picked them up quickly. He may not have wanted another stuffed whale but I definitely wanted another bag of those sour gummy worms. Or another ring.

"My mom knows something," he said again, walking over to the air-hockey table. "I just don't know what it is."

He put in a token, dropped the puck. I picked up the red striker and slid it across. "Why can't school teach us about this? Like how to uncover secrets from parents who think you're too young to know the truth?"

"You're thinking of spy school," I said with complete certainty.

Brett slammed the puck. It went straight into my goal. Dammit.

"How is knowing about atoms and molecules going to help me stop my family from falling apart?"

"Well, technically that's the point of atoms. They build stuff, keep everything together." I looked up. He was giving me a look. I used the opportunity to slam the puck into his goal. "What? I'm in AP Bio."

Brett snorted. Then he started chuckling. Then he was doubled over, completely out of control. He dropped onto the floor with his back against the table and kept laughing.

I thought he'd officially lost it.

I sat beside him. Our legs bumped against each other's. I remembered what it felt like when he said he had a crush on me, the way his lips parted when we kissed at Lovers' Lake. And I really wished I was a detective because maybe then I could figure out the mystery that was my heart and whatever these feelings blooming inside me were.

"You know the term 'climax'?" I asked.

"Yes. But I think it's a different 'climax' than you're referencing."

I set myself up for that one.

Ignoring him, I said, "Miss Copper was talking about it during class yesterday. Basically in every book, there's a sequence of events that happens to build up to one monumental moment. That's called 'rising action.' It leads up to the story's climax, which is, like, the most intense moment, when something crazy happens and the reader is left in shock. Like the characters break up, a secret is revealed—that sort of thing."

"Oh, Becca. I love it when you get all geeky."

I swatted his arm.

"The point is that after the climax, the final stage of a book is the resolution. It's where all the problems are solved, the characters are happy again, and there's this sense of relief, Brett. What's happening right now with your family? Think of it as the climax, when everything gets crazy. What I'm trying to say is that you need to hang in a little longer, wait for the resolution. Because then, everything will be okay. *You'll* be okay."

Brett put his arm around my shoulder. "You're kind of amazing, Becca Hart," he said. I started to laugh before I saw the serious look on his face. No teasing this time, no poking fun. He really meant that.

The butterflies were back.

I shrugged, fidgeting with the hem of my shirt. "I told you to pay attention in English."

"Why pay attention when I'm dating the smartest girl in class? You're like my own personal textbook."

"Wow, I am so flattered. Is that all you like me for?"

"No," he said. "Not at all." Then he quickly jumped up and tugged me to my feet with him. The tickets all fell out of his pocket but he didn't care. He held on to my hands, forcing me to face him. He had that crazy look in his eyes again. This time he was smiling. One hundred watts and all. "Come to the hotel's opening with me this weekend." He said it all in one breath.

I mean, I kind of thought I was already supposed to go, being his fake girlfriend and all. "Sure," I said anyway.

"No, Becca. Not like some fake date where we spend the night pretending and hold hands because people expect us to. A real date this time. Me and you. . . . Would you want that? Do you want to come with me?"

My heart had grown wings and soared out of my chest. "I—"

"I want you there. I think I need you there. And for one night, let's stop doing things because we have to, okay? Can we do that and see what happens?"

I could feel the chains around my heart loosening. It was

wiggling free, inch by inch. I tried to lock it back up but it wasn't so easy to restrain anymore.

Oh, whatever. I took the chains off.

"Yeah," I told Brett. "Yeah we can."

The hotel's grand opening was way too glamourous for Crestmont, a town that always smelled a little like sewage. This party was better suited for an old Hollywood movie.

It was being held in the hotel's lobby. The floors were marble, and you could hear the sound of women's heels tip-tapping along. Waiters were floating around too, carrying flutes of champagne and hors d'oeuvres that I wasn't entirely sure how to eat. I felt like Ariel in that scene from *The Little Mermaid* where she uses a fork for a hairbrush. Like I'd been picked up from my life as Becca Hart and dropped into an alternate universe of lavish food and expensive gowns. Two things I knew nothing about. If it weren't for Brett smiling at my side, the entire night would have felt like a dream.

To be fair, Brett may have made this even *more* dreamlike. As soon as I thought he had reached his peak level of attractiveness, he put on a suit and blew my freaking mind.

His parents surprised me the most. I was still so deep in detective mode that I had expected his dad to be secretive and guarded, like those villains in movies that suspiciously stand in corners and watch the crowd. I thought his mom would have this sadness lurking beneath the surface, the same way mine used to. Instead they were all wide smiles, nonstop hand holding, and dressed to the nines. And I got what Brett meant by not being able to figure out the truth. From an outsider's perspective, his family appeared picture perfect.

"Having fun?" Brett's voice in my ear made me jump. He put his hands on my hips and it had a different effect on me now. Knowing that we weren't pretending tonight changed everything.

"This place looks incredible," I said.

"Right? I feel like we're not even in Crestmont anymore. Or Georgia. You still have to meet my parents," he said. His mom and dad had been so busy talking to all the guests that Brett hadn't had a chance to introduce me yet. I was feeling more nervous by the minute.

"Where are they?" I asked.

Brett pushed my hips a little until I was facing the other side of the room. A bar had been set up along a wall entirely of windows. It looked like it led to an outdoor seating area. He pointed toward his parents, who were talking to another man and woman. "See that couple?" he said. "The woman is an interior designer. She did all the decorating."

"Wow. Where'd they come from? New York?" There

was no way this style was inspired by Georgia. There was too much glam and not enough comfort.

Brett grabbed what looked like a mini hot dog off a waiter's tray and popped it into his mouth. "They live here," he said. "You don't recognize them?"

I looked a little closer, tried to see behind the glitz and glamour. Then I remembered their faces from years ago. "They're the McHenrys," I said. "Jenny's parents." As if on cue, Jenny walked right up to the bar and stood beside them.

"For the record, I didn't know she'd be here until this moment. . . . You can meet my parents later," he said, reading my mind. "Let's go get some air."

Brett led me through the crowd and out a set of glass doors. There was a small outdoor patio overlooking the pool that we were standing on. With the moon high in the sky and the humidity nowhere to be found, it was the perfect night. And it was quiet. So quiet. I could hear how quickly my heart was beating.

We were leaning against the railing, staring out into the darkness. Brett's eyes shifted to me, then down to my toes. "I like your dress," he said. His fingers reached out, touching my ironed curls. "And I like your hair when it's like this." Then he grabbed my hand, pulling me against his chest. "And I like us like this. Without the pretending."

"Me too."

Brett smiled. His eyes crinkled at the corners. "You do?"

"Yeah." Maybe it was the darkness or the quiet that made my lips a little bit looser, because then I was saying, "I like you, Brett. Which was never supposed to happen. That's why I was okay with our relationship being fake, because it was safe. It was supposed to prevent all of this so I wouldn't have to worry about getting my heart broken. And now we're here and everything feels too real and it's scaring me."

"Tell me why you're scared," he said.

"Because relationships never work out. Look at my parents. I always thought they were so in love, that they'd last forever, and then one morning my dad woke up and decided that we weren't enough. That his life wasn't enough. People always talk about falling in love but no one ever talks about falling *out* of it. And look at your parents—" Brett flinched. "Sorry. Forget that. I don't know. It's like I said, people always leave. Parents, friends—it doesn't matter. It's all temporary and I'm not sure I can handle another person walking out on me."

"Then let me show you that I can be the one who stays."

"As sweet as that is, Brett, there's no way you can know for sure you'll even want to. Relationships are just one big gamble where the odds are always against you. And on a night like this, when I'm wearing a dress for the first time in years and it feels like we're in an entirely different world? It's easy to get caught up in the moment. To over-romanticize the little things."

"You're saying you think I'm going to, what, wake up tomorrow and decide that I don't actually have feelings for you?" he asked. I nodded. "That's impossible, Becca. I started feeling like this way before tonight. And I promise you I'll feel this way tomorrow too, and the days after that." Brett touched his finger to my forehead. "You're stuck in your own mind, overthinking this too much and looking for every fault. There doesn't always have to be a negative side."

"I'm confused," I said, "because one day we were strangers and then, bam, we were pretending to be in love. All these lines between what was real and what was fake started to blur and I can't tell the two apart anymore."

"Just because we were pretending doesn't mean it wasn't real," Brett said.

Maybe he was right. That day we kissed in the hallway had changed something inside me, dredging up all these feelings I never wanted to feel. We were pretending to date one day, then secretly being friends the next. Somewhere in the middle of all that—between our time spent at the arcade and sharing secrets in his car—fake became real and I was too busy ignoring my own heart to even realize it.

But maybe I didn't want to ignore it anymore.

Maybe it was time to undo the locks and open all the windows. Maybe falling in love didn't mean you were doomed and the future couldn't be determined by the past. Maybe I had to stop living my life through books and it was time to rip off all the caution tape and see what happened when I let myself feel. Or when I let myself fall.

And I wanted to feel everything with Brett.

"Brett?"

"Becca?"

I leaned my head into his chest. "Don't break my heart. Okay?"

His hand tilted up my chin until our eyes met. He was all shadows and moonlight.

"I won't," he said.

Right when Brett was about to kiss me, the patio doors opened and a woman stepped out. The only thing that kept her black outfit from blending into the night was the silver camera hanging from her neck. "There you are! Can I get a photo of you two?" she asked, lip ring catching the moonlight. Brett was groaning at the interruption. "Can I get you to turn a little so the moon is behind you? That's perfect. Smile!" she yelled before the flash went off. She didn't need to tell us, though. I couldn't seem to stop smiling. She looked down at the camera and nodded her approval, lifting her eyes back to ours. "Great. You two make a cute couple." She walked away and the words were there, floating around.

That was the first time someone thought we were a couple when we weren't pretending to be one.

From the way we were facing, I could see down the side of the hotel. There was a small path that led to a side entrance to the building and eventually opened up into the parking lot. It was dark, but the lamps created enough light for me to make out that someone was standing there, behind a car, in a way that it would block anyone looking from another angle from seeing them. I could see their face, though.

"Brett," I whispered. "Look." He followed my eyes to his father. Then, while we both watched, a woman stepped out from behind the car. Only it wasn't Brett's mom. There was no mistaking it this time. No more clues worth searching for. The answer was right in front of us.

"It's the same woman from the diner," he breathed.

I peeled my eyes away to find Brett. So many emotions flickered across his face like a slideshow. First surprise. Then sadness. It ended with anger. He let go of my waist and his hands balled into fists. His eyes looked as dark as the sky, not a star in sight.

The rest happened too fast. Brett was walking down the path, then he was running. I chased after him, yelled his name. He was too tall, his footsteps too quick. Then he was standing in front of his dad, yelling. I watched the woman's eyes go wide. His dad's were wider.

"You brought her here!" he was screaming, waving his arms around. "To this hotel with Mom right inside?"

It was like watching a car crash. I couldn't look away.

His dad's mouth was moving but there were no words coming out. It made sense—what was there to say in this moment? There was no excuse to make this better. There was only the truth and the aftermath.

Then Brett was crying and I reached for him, placed my hands on his shoulder. "I saw you at the diner," he was saying. "I didn't want to believe it, Dad. That you'd do this to Mom. That you'd lie to us for all this time and spend all those weekends away from home—and for what? For *her*?"

I looked at the woman for the first time. She had her hands covering her face. I thought she was crying, but then I realized she was shocked. This was all a surprise to her. She was looking between Brett and his dad like she too was putting her own puzzle together. Did she not know she was dating a married man?

"Brett," I said, trying to pull him toward me. His feet were lead. The doors to the hotel swung open and a stream of people poured out, coming to check on all the noise. The four of us were standing there, covered in tears, with just enough moonlight to illuminate the truth for everyone to see. I saw Brett's mother at the front. She walked toward us, stopped right beside me.

"What happened?" she said. I watched her face fall as she gazed between her husband and his mistress, and then it felt like I was standing on my father's driveway all over again, trying to keep it together when the world was tearing me apart.

I had never seen someone look more broken than when Brett turned to face his mom. But she didn't look surprised, not like the mistress did. And in that moment, we both realized that his mom had known all along. Her face was not one of a woman who'd just found out her marriage had been a lie. It was the face of a woman who had kept a secret that was now out in the open.

Brett almost fell over. His hand reached out and grabbed the car and I was there, holding him up as much as I could, but he was too heavy for me to carry on my own.

"You knew?" he said, looking at his mom. "You knew all this time?"

The five of us stood there in silence. The crowd was watching, waiting for a show. And with a town as small as Crestmont, Brett's parents would be talked about all over town tomorrow morning. The curtain had fallen on their perfect family and this was all that was left.

The look on his mom's face reminded me of my mom's,

that kind of heartbreak that eats at you slowly, tearing you apart. I understood why she hadn't told Brett. It was the same reason my mom turned to baking. They were just trying to hold it together, contain the heartbreak in their own chests and not let it spread to their children.

But Brett couldn't see that right now. He was too angry.

"You knew," he said again, louder this time. "And you"—he spun around to face his dad—"how could you do this?" His voice broke. I thought he was going to cry, to collapse completely. Instead he lunged. His fist connected with his father's face in a horrifying sound. His dad was on the ground, clutching his nose, blood streaming down.

My mouth was hanging open.

I stared at Brett with blood on his fist.

I stared at his dad with blood on his face.

I stared at his mom and the other woman, who were both crying.

Then I grabbed Brett's hand and this time I was the one pulling him away. We ran through the parking lot and I ignored the way my feet ached in my heels. I took a left down the street on a whim and we kept walking until Brett fell over onto the grass. He was lying there, face to the sky, bloody hand clutched in his chest.

I sat down.

It was so quiet. Not even a car drove by.

I looked down at my dress and saw the blood on it. Brett must have heard me gasp because he started apologizing. "I'm sorry. I'm so sorry, Becca."

I pulled his head onto my chest, ignoring his bloody hands. "It's okay. It'll be okay," I said. But this time I wasn't entirely sure.

"I shouldn't have done that. I shouldn't have punched him but he deserved it—and my mom. Oh my god, my mom. Did you see her face?" He was crying again. "She knew, Becca. She knew this whole time and didn't tell me."

"You're angry at your dad, Brett. Not your mom. She's in as much pain as you are."

He stood up, wiped his tears. "I have to go back," he declared. "I can't leave her there with him." He began walking back down the sidewalk. I ran after him, grabbed his arm, and spun him around.

"No," I said. "What you need is to stay here. I'll go get your mom if that's what you want, but you can't go back there, Brett. Not like this. You're too angry. You're not thinking straight. And you're going to do something much worse than punch him this time."

Brett was breathing heavy. I tried to read his face and failed. But I knew what he was feeling. I was no stranger to the confusion, the guilt, the sadness—the way all three of them mixed into one gigantic mess until you couldn't decipher what was what anymore.

"My dad deserved that," Brett said, sounding angry.

"He did. I know he did. But all those people didn't need to see it. You know how they talk—"

"I don't care what people say about my family or what they're going to think, Becca! My dad's a liar. Everything has been a fucking lie! Shouldn't people know that? Why should his image be protected?"

"That's not what I meant. At all. This," I said, gesturing back to the hotel, "is already going to be hard enough without the entire town's opinions weighing in."

There was no getting through to Brett now. His mind was made up. "I'm going to get my mom," he said. "Please don't try to stop me."

So I didn't. I let him walk away and then I lay down on the grass. It was damp, a little cold. It was probably going to stain my dress green, which didn't matter since it was already stained red. Remembering the blood, I scrubbed at the fabric with my thumb, but it was too late. That was the thing with blood; it stained. Whether it was there for a second or a minute, you couldn't get rid of it. It soaked itself into the fabric so deeply that it became a part of it.

I raised my head off the grass and stared down the sidewalk, toward the hotel. A car was driving this way. It had to be Brett and his mom. I sat up, brushed myself off, and walked to the side of the road. The car pulled over, the window rolled down, and it was the last person I expected.

"Becca?" Jenny asked, staring down at the mess I had become. "You look like you could use a ride."

Brett

OUR HOUSE WAS SILENT.

My mom was asleep in her bedroom. She stopped crying sometime after midnight. After I went back to the hotel to get her, the entire crowd that had gathered was gone. The parking lot was empty. Like everything was a bad dream. I found my mom sitting on a couch in the lobby. She had her arms wrapped around herself like she was physically trying to not fall apart. There was makeup smudged down her face. My dad was standing at the bar, surrounded by hotel staff. He looked completely fine. Still put together. I ignored him and grabbed my mom. She didn't speak, didn't say a single word. I held her up and walked us to my car.

"I'm sorry." She kept repeating those two words for the entire drive home. That's what hurt me the most. That she thought this was her fault.

"You don't have to be," I told her. There was nothing else to say.

My mom had a death grip on my arm as we walked from the car to the front door, like I was her anchor in all of this. I didn't know how to tell her I was drowning too.

I brought her to bed and wiped the makeup off her face with a warm towel. I tucked her in, pulled the blanket right up to her chin like she used to do for me. I kissed her forehead. "I love you," I said. I thought back to what Becca said about the climax and the resolution. The calm after this storm. "We're going to be okay, Mom."

She opened her eyes, placed her hand on my cheek. "I wanted to protect you," she said.

"You did. But now we'll protect each other." I wouldn't let her carry this on her own anymore.

I sat on the edge of the bed until she fell asleep. It didn't take long, maybe a few minutes. When her face looked peaceful again, I left and went back downstairs. I sat on the couch and waited. I didn't take my eyes off the door. He had to be on his way home. Any second, he'd walk inside.

An hour later the door opened.

My dad was standing in the doorway, his tie hanging loose around his neck. I was still trying to adjust to all of this. When you've spent seventeen years thinking you know someone, how are you supposed to train yourself to see them differently? I'd looked up to him for so long. I wanted to be like him. I wanted to learn from him. I wanted to impress him. And now what? How was I supposed to just shut that off? The anger was still swirling inside me, a neighbor to the sadness, but there was relief there too when I saw him. Because he was my dad. He was supposed to be the one protecting me. He was supposed to tell me what to do now, where we went from here.

Instead I was left alone, trying to separate my dad from the person standing in the hallway. And I couldn't.

All the lights in the house were off so he didn't see me sitting on the couch. He started walking up the stairs. What was he going to do? Jump into bed with my mom and sleep beside her? Then we'd wake up tomorrow morning and have one big family breakfast?

Didn't he realize that everything was different now?

My voice cut through the darkness. "You can't stay here." His footsteps faltered. "Not anymore. Not with Mom here."

My dad looked different as he walked into the living room. Maybe it was the blood covering his white shirt or the broken nose and the fresh purple bruises. Everyone always told me I looked like my dad more than my mom. Now? I couldn't find a trace of myself in his face.

He sat down, took off his glasses, and rubbed his eyes. He looked exhausted. Not sad. Not guilty. Just tired, like the truth finally coming out was this huge interruption from his regularly scheduled life.

"Let me explain," he said.

And then the weirdest thing happened. I didn't want him to.

I was sitting there in the middle of the night and all I could think about was Becca and how she spent five years with all these questions that were never answered. And here I was, every answer within reach, and none of it even mattered. Because there was no explanation. There was no excuse. Whatever reason my dad had for cheating wouldn't make me forgive him. Not if he spent the rest of the night apologizing. All I knew was that my mom had been completely embarrassed tonight and spending another second talking to the person behind it felt wrong.

What good was the truth when it was too late for it?

I didn't care what the woman's name was, where she lived, how they met, or if she had kids. There was really only one question I wanted to know.

"How long has this been going on?"

"Three months," my dad said.

"How long has Mom known?"

"She found out in August."

I felt so damn useless. How long had I spent obsessing over football to impress my dad? Practicing day and night? I even dragged Becca into this, agreed to date her to impress him too. And for what? For him to miss every game this season? For him to be off living this second life? And I just sat here and let him. I was too blinded by trying to be him, pick up his life from where he had left off, that I couldn't even realize he was the last person I ever wanted to be.

I got up and walked out of the room, pausing at the stairs. "You can't stay here anymore," I said again. Without waiting for a response, I left my father there on the couch. I didn't go to bed until I heard the front door open and close, then the sound of his car leaving. For a second I thought that maybe he'd go stay with this other woman. But it didn't matter anymore. None of it did.

Everything felt tainted. Dirty. I and all my hobbies were extensions of my dad. And now I couldn't figure out what parts of myself were really *me*. Like football; did I even enjoy playing it? Was it all to impress my dad? Would I have started playing on my own if he hadn't forced a football into my hands when I was a kid? Then there was Becca. That was the worst part. Our entire relationship began because of how desperate I was to please my dad. I knew it had grown from that, but it still felt wrong that he was the reason for everything good that had happened and everything bad.

I didn't know what to do, where to go from here.

I felt like what I needed was a fresh start. A clean slate to figure out who I was without him.

Becca

THE NEXT MORNING PLAYED OUT in a strange series of events.

I woke up in my bed, that was normal. I was still wearing the dress. There was enough sunlight coming in through the blinds to confirm that, yes, there was still blood on it and yes, there was still blood on my fingertips. Another sign that last night really happened and wasn't a weird dream my brain concocted while I was asleep.

I winced thinking of the punch, felt this weird tightness in my chest at the memory of Brett walking away from me. And then there was the weirdest part of all, Jenny. I remember accepting her ride home and crawling into bed that night. But I didn't remember what happened between that.

It was like my brain decided to completely shut down due to information overload.

There was a knock at my door. My mom stuck her head in. "Good, you're awake." She walked inside, opened all the blinds even when I protested, and grabbed clothing out of my dresser. She said, "Get up, take a shower, and come have breakfast. There's someone waiting to see you," then left before I could ask who it was. But it could only be one person: Brett. Which meant he was currently sitting alone in my kitchen with my mom.

I never showered so fast.

Ten minutes later the bloody dress was in the hamper, red stains on my skin were gone, and my hair no longer smelled like grass. I walked into the kitchen in a rush because Brett had already spent way too much time alone with my mother and I had to intervene as soon as possible. Only it wasn't Brett sitting at my kitchen table. It was Jenny.

I froze halfway through the doorway. They both turned at the same time to stare at me. I felt like an animal in a zoo exhibit. *What will Becca do now?*

"Are you hungry?" my mom asked like this was a normal breakfast setup. "I made you banana pancakes. Your favorite." They were my favorite, but I was too confused to even think about eating.

"Jenny came over," my mom continued when it was clear I wasn't going to speak. "She told me what happened with Brett's family last night. It's terrible. I hope he's all right."

Great. So the news was slowly making its way around Crestmont.

"I wanted to make sure you were okay," Jenny said. Note to self: a town tragedy was what it took to have Jenny speak to me again. "You seemed to be a little in shock last night. You didn't say a word the entire drive here."

My brain was still struggling to understand this breakfast dynamic when my mom checked her watch and made a big show of standing up. "I have to get to the bakery. Will you ladies be all right here?" I think I nodded because she kept going. "And Becca, if you talk to Brett, tell him he's welcome to come here whenever. I don't think his house is where he wants to be right now."

"Sure, Mom. Thanks."

Then she left. It was awkward without her to fill the silence, be the middle man.

Jenny spoke first. "I always liked your mom," she said. There was a half-eaten jelly bell on her plate. "It's cool that she tries to be involved in your life. . . ." Her eyes met mine. "Her baking improved a lot too. I still didn't really believe it until I ate this."

"Why are you here?" It came out harsher than intended.

And okay, I should probably at least *try* to be a little nicer to her. I mean, she did kind of save me from being stranded on the road last night.

"I told you. I wanted to make sure you were okay after last night."

"But why?"

Her face scrunched up. "Am I not allowed to still care about you? We were best friends."

"Two years ago," I pointed out.

Jenny stood up in a hurry. "Coming here was a mistake. I'll leave."

"Jenny, wait." I held my face in my hands. She sat back down. "I'm sorry, okay? Don't go. . . . I'm just trying to make sense of this. Last night and now this morning? Nothing feels normal anymore."

"I know," she said softly. "That's why I came here. Figured you could use some sense of familiarity. And . . ." Her words trailed off.

"And what?" I asked, wanting the distraction.

"And you were right. I wasn't a good friend to you. I haven't been for a long time. And, like, I don't expect us to become besties overnight or whatever. But maybe, eventually, we can be okay again. . . ." Jenny sighed. "I just feel bad. What you said at the marsh made me realize how selfish I had become. And the worst part is that I don't even know when I became like this. So, fine, I'm trying to make it up to you. Repent for my sins or whatever."

Surprisingly, this confession wasn't the weirdest thing that had happened to me in the past twenty-four hours. And maybe it was because of how much my life had changed recently, but suddenly the thought of reconciling with Jenny didn't seem all that crazy.

"Have you spoken to Brett?" she added.

I'd been in such a rush to barge into the kitchen I'd forgotten to even check my phone.

"No," I said quickly. "Not yet. Why? Got any advice?"

Jenny laughed, ate the other half of the jelly bell. "No. Not this time. It's weird, right? His family is, like, worshipped in this town or something. Goes to show that every family has their secrets. What?" She grabbed a napkin and wiped her mouth. "Is there sugar on my face?"

"No. It's just— It's weird seeing you here. But it feels normal at the same time. Does that make sense?"

"Tell me about it. It was weird coming here two years later. I wasn't sure if I even should come, but you seemed *really* not okay last night, Becca. Like, your mind was in a different world or something. Without the book this time."

I sat down at the table across from her. "My life is starting to feel like one."

We both laughed. For that second, it was like the past two years never happened and we were two fifteen-year-old best friends again.

"Do you hear that?" she asked, glancing around the kitchen. "It sounds like a phone ringing." It was a phone. My phone. I ran to my bedroom to grab it. Brett's name was on the screen. I let out a huge sigh of relief.

"Brett, hey. How are you?"

"Are you home?" His voice was muffled. It sounded like he was driving with the windows down. I told him I was. "Can I come over? I need to talk to you."

"Of course."

I hung up and ran back to the kitchen.

"Brett?"

I nodded. "He's on his way."

"Guess that's my cue to leave." Jenny stood up and we walked to the door. I had to restrain myself from opening it and shooing her out. I wanted to talk to Brett. I needed to know he was okay. But then Jenny turned back around, looking like she was debating whether or not to say something. "I, um, hope everything's okay with him. My dad and his dad are friends. I don't want it to be weird when people start choosing sides."

I must've said something because she waved and left. She

was halfway down the hall when I called her name. "The hotel looked great, by the way. Brett told me your parents furnished it."

Jenny used to have this huge smile before it turned tight-lipped. The kind that completely took over her entire face. I hadn't seen it since freshman year. Until now. "Thanks, Becca," she said.

The elevator doors opened and Brett walked out. He glanced between me and Jenny, looking confused, said something to her, then kept walking. "What was that about?" he asked once he was in front of me. He looked disheveled. It was clear he hadn't slept.

"Long story. How was last night?" I reached out and wrapped my arms around him. He patted my back a few times, then let go. I looked up at him. His face was unreadable. "Brett? Is everything okay?"

He wouldn't look me in the eyes. "Can we talk?"

"Sure."

I gazed at the door for a moment, twirling the key around in my hand. It felt too private, bringing Brett inside when no one else was there. So I made my way to the elevator, knowing he'd follow, and pressed the button to the roof. We didn't speak as we rode up, and Brett trailed behind as I walked over to lean on the cement ledge overlooking the town. He stood beside me, his side against mine. It wasn't normal, what that did to my heart.

I waited for him to grab my hand like he usually did when we were side by side.

"I used to come here as a kid," I explained.

"To read?"

I rolled my eyes. "No. Not to read. To think. There was something about standing up here that made my problems shrink, made the world feel a little bit smaller. A little less scary." I glanced at him. He was nodding along. "You're being really quiet."

Brett looked the same as he did last night. Still angry. Still a little confused. His eyes were scanning the town below us like he'd find answers written in the rooftops.

He may have looked the same, but he felt far away.

"My dad came home late last night," he said. "I told him to leave, that he couldn't stay there with me and Mom."

"Did he explain what happened with that woman?"

"You mean his mistress?" he said, gripping the ledge a little tighter. "He wanted to but I wouldn't let him."

"You didn't want answers?" That made zero sense to me. I'd give anything for a few explanations.

"I thought I did until he was sitting in front of me. Then I realized that it doesn't matter anymore, Becca.

Answers, the truth, whatever you want to call it. None of it matters because it's too late. Nothing he says will fix what he's done to my mom, to our family. Maybe there's some truths that are better kept as secrets." His head fell into his hands. "This sucks. This really sucks. My mom didn't get out of bed this morning. She thinks I can't hear her crying but I can."

I wanted to tell him how sorry I was, but I knew all too well that my sympathy wouldn't take away a fraction of the pain. They were empty words, like trying to use a single Band-Aid to hold an entire shattered heart together.

So I reached through the space between us and held his hand. The wind blew a strand of hair onto his forehead and I brushed it away, waiting for him to continue.

Brett let out a long breath. "I'm sorry for leaving you last night," he said.

"It's okay. Jenny gave me a ride."

Now that caught his attention. "You guys are friends again?"

Were we? "I'm not really sure."

He nodded, staring back at the sky. "I didn't come here just to talk about my family. I want to talk about us."

It was selfish, but I perked up at this. Until he let go of my hand.

"I've been thinking," Brett continued, "that so much of

my life was based off my dad. I started playing football for him. I based all my plans for college off what he wanted me to do or what he would have done. I always felt like it was my responsibility to live the life he wanted for me. Like it was my fault for being born and taking those opportunities away from him. It's weird to think about, but it feels like my life hasn't really been mine. I don't even know if I *like* football, Becca. Or if I convinced myself I did because I had no other choice."

I wasn't following. "You're going to quit the team?"

"No. I can't do that to my teammates." Then he finally turned away from the sky to look at me. I wished he hadn't. His eyes held all the truths. "You remember why we both agreed to start dating? How I did it for my dad?" I nodded, knowing where this was heading. "That was just another thing I did for him. And I don't want us to be like that. I don't want our story to start because of him. Everything in my life has happened because of my dad and I need one thing to feel like mine."

"I don't understand." But I did understand. I just didn't want to.

"I think we need to break up. Stop this fake relationship for a little. I just need some time to think. Some space."

My first reaction was to laugh because I couldn't believe people actually used that line in real life. Then the words sank in and my throat started to tighten, the way it did before I cried. "But last night," I said, thinking back to our conversation on the patio, "you said you wanted to be together. You said it felt real even when we were pretending. You said you wouldn't leave."

"I know." Now he reached for my hands. His eyes were begging. I took a step back, letting his fingers grasp air. "I meant what I said. I meant every word of it. It felt real, it all did. But that was before everything changed, Becca. Now my head is a mess and it's like I can't separate what feelings were really mine."

"So this is your solution? To end this?"

Brett took another step closer. "Please don't cry."

It only made me cry harder. I felt so stupid. Five years—five years I had spent locking everyone out because I thought it was for the best. Because I knew I couldn't handle another person walking out on me. And all it took was one night for me to change my mind, to decide that maybe it would be okay to let someone in. Especially if that person was Brett. I *wanted* that person to be Brett. But he didn't want to be that person. And I couldn't make him either.

The tears were falling now. My face was hot with embarrassment. I wanted to run inside. This entire day was a disaster and I'd only just woken up.

I took a deep breath, then said, "I'm sorry about your

father. I really am, Brett. I know what it feels like to be let down by a parent, believe me. I've spent the past five years feeling like that. But I also know what it feels like to run from it and to want to lock everyone out. It doesn't work. It makes everything worse."

"Becca—"

"I think you should leave."

"I'm sorry," he said again. "I never wanted any of this to happen."

"I know," I said, and I think that was the problem. That his feelings for me weren't enough to stand out in all this mess, when my feelings for him were all that stood out in mine.

When it was clear Brett wasn't going anywhere, I was the one who left. I stepped into the elevator and watched him disappear as the doors closed. It brought back memories of my father leaving. I remembered what it felt like to wake up to an empty home. I remembered what it felt like when Jenny stopped caring about our friendship. These memories I tried so hard to block out were resurfacing. I was starting to drown in them.

But this time I wouldn't let myself. Because this time was different.

This time, I was the one walking away.

* * *

My feelings began to change as the week dragged on. Apparently hiding out in my bedroom was not an appropriate way to deal with whatever this feeling was. (Rejection? Heartbreak? A little bit of each?) Dodging Brett at school was beginning to take a toll on my physical health. It was exhausting having to peek into every hallway and eat lunch behind the football field just to avoid seeing him. And, okay, maybe avoiding him wasn't the best solution, but what did I know? Relationship virgin here. Even books didn't prepare me for this.

Speaking of books, that's where I had begun to direct all my anger. I stopped feeling sorry for myself and created a mental reminder to stop putting all the blame on Brett. He was going through a lot with his family right now. It wasn't fair to expect him to prioritize me in all this chaos. So instead I put all the blame, again, on these books that were lighthearted and fun. They were about people falling in love in beach houses and amusement parks, where their only worry was melting ice cream. There was nothing in those pages about fake relationships. Or what to do when the fake world you created came crashing down around you. Why couldn't I find a book on how to deal with a very fake—yet very real—breakup?

Where were the books on that, huh?

The worst part was the amount of time I wasted reading

these things and losing myself in fantasies that were never going to happen. And at the beginning, that was the point. To read something so completely outrageous and find comfort in the fact that the fictional love and heartbreak would never happen to me. But it wasn't even worth it because it *did* happen to me. I was left standing here with all these books and a broken heart from a boy I never really even dated.

I was a colossal mess.

My mom walked into my room while I was staring at my bookshelf. When I was nearly done with my internal rant, she cleared her throat. "What are you doing?" she asked. "Thinking about what to read next?"

I shook my head. "Thinking about which to throw away, actually. Maybe I'll burn them, watch the romance go up in flames. That could be cool."

My mom actually gasped. "But you love these books!"

"I *loved* them." Past tense.

"Oh, baby. What happened?" she asked, tugging me onto my bed. I guess I could have told her about Brett. She'd know what to say. But I couldn't do it. My mom had spent all my teenage years asking me about boys, waiting for her daughter to fall in love and have some grand, fairy-tale romance. It never happened. I knew she thought that I wasn't really living my life to the fullest, which was all she ever wanted. I just . . . I wasn't sure how to tell her that I finally met someone and it started off fake and then, when it was beginning to feel real, it got ruined. Completely freaking messed up. Catastrophic chaos.

"I don't want to talk about it," I said.

I expected her to fight me on this and declare some unofficial mother-daughter therapy session. Instead she patted my back and walked out of the room.

"Something's up," I heard her whisper once the door was closed. "She's talking about burning her books."

"Not the books!" Cassie yelled. Side note: Since when was Cassie here? This better not be some sort of intervention.

"I can hear you two!" I called back. The door burst open and Cassie barged through. I think she was trying to seem threatening but it was kind of ruined by the powdered sugar all over her face.

"This better not be about Brett breaking up with you," she said, pointing her finger at me very aggressively. "I've waited too long for you to have feelings for literally anyone and now that it happens, you're moping around like some tragic heroine."

"I'm not a tragic heroine."

"You are. The super annoying type that won't tell anyone how they feel. Not their mom, or even their best friend. Super lame, Becca. The books are ashamed of you. Can you hear them crying? Can you? Look what you're doing to them." She jumped onto my bed, full face-plant, and sighed dramatically. I had to fight back the giggles.

Reluctantly, I took a seat beside her. "This isn't about Brett," I said. Cassie gave me a look. "Fine. It may be partially about Brett, but only, like, twenty percent."

"How about the other eighty percent?"

"The books," I said. "I feel like they're mocking me." Cassie slapped her hand over my forehead. "What are you doing?"

"Checking if you have a fever."

I pushed her hand away. "The only thing making me sick is staring at these books all day long. With their stupid, false happy endings. It's a scam. The entire book industry is a gigantic scam, Cassie. Why doesn't anyone talk about this? How is this legal? They're feeding vulnerable readers lies about love and life and we're buying into it like mindless consumers."

Cassie stood up. "Amy!" My mom appeared in the doorway. She was obviously eavesdropping. "You need to take it from here," Cassie said before walking out of the room.

Then I had an idea. I ran to the kitchen and rummaged through the cabinets until I found the box of garbage bags, the extra-large ones my mom uses for recycling.

"What is she doing?" Cassie mumbled.

"No idea."

I ignored the two of them and marched back to my bedroom. Then I shut the door and took as many books as I could off the shelves and threw them into the bag. I started off with the cheesiest ones, the ones with the happiest endings and the promises of eternal love. Yuck. Then I did the same with the ones that had made me cry. Then the ones that I didn't really like but still read anyway because it was physically impossible for me to stop reading a book halfway. When the bag was full and half the bookshelf was empty, I tied the top, lifted it into my arms, and walked out of my apartment.

"Where are you taking those?" my mom called after me.

"Don't follow me!" I yelled back. "Either of you!"

By some miracle, they didn't. I guess there was something about a slightly sleep-deprived teenager shoving books into a bag that scared people off.

I marched to the elevator, pressed the button to the lobby, and waited. My arms were beginning to ache from the weight of all these books, but I didn't care. It was nice to feel that weight somewhere other than my heart.

I was sitting with my feet dangling over the edge of the bridge, the water lapping beneath me. It made me think of the night I spent at Lovers' Lake with Brett. The kiss, the piggyback rides, the moonlight reflecting off the lake—it all seemed so perfect at the time.

Stupid books. Nothing prepared me for this.

The weird part was that my heart didn't feel entirely broken. Not the way it had after the divorce. Now it was like, instead of the entire thing shattering, just one tiny little piece of it was missing. A subtle ache. But it was there all the same. And it still hurt.

It was my fault for getting my hopes up. Because before I met Brett, love was an idea I was fine reading about. It existed on pages, and that was okay because that was safe. Then I saw it begin to take shape between us. And I think part of me began to feel that maybe this entire idea of love wasn't so bad after all. Maybe my parents just had a bad experience. Right? Maybe, for other people, it could actually work. Maybe Brett and I were two of those people it could work for.

With hindsight, I realized now I was wrong. I should have remained pessimistic and kept all the locks and chains around my heart.

Now there was only one thing left to do.

I reached into the bag and blindly chose a book. I didn't even look at it, I just opened it to a random page, tore it out, then threw it into the water. I watched it float, then slowly move away. I breathed, counted to five, then threw the entire book in. Now it sank, right down to the very bottom until I could no longer see it. Good. I didn't want to see it. Seeing was a reminder. I wanted it gone.

I grabbed another book and threw it into the water. Then another. And another. I sat there under the sun until the bag was half empty, the lake a little fuller. I was tearing through a book about a dying girl in Maine when Jenny appeared out of nowhere. She was standing beside me, breathing too loud. Or maybe I had gotten used to the quiet.

"God, Becca. What are you doing?" she asked. I ignored her and threw another one in. "You're polluting the water."

I threw another, then said, "Semi-broken hearts are selfish. They don't care about things like pollution."

Jenny sat beside me, her flip-flop-clad feet dangling over the edge. Her toenails were painted bright yellow. "I heard about you and Brett," she said. "I'm sorry."

"Thanks," I mumbled. There was nothing else to say. I picked up another book and threw it in, not even bothering to look at the title.

Then Jenny held out her hand, palm toward the sky. I stared at it for a minute, then her smiling face. It made sense that she was so popular. She was beautiful, like that natural kind of beauty that made you wonder how it was even possible for someone to look like that. I searched her face, looking for the friend I used to know.

"Give me a book," she said.

So I did. She scanned the cover, flipped it over a few times, then asked, "This is the one you were reading that morning. Right?"

I snorted. "The one you made fun of? No. This one's different."

"They all look the same. What's the story?" she asked, gently tapping the book against her thigh.

"Isn't it always about love?"

"I mean *your* story," she corrected me. "When did you buy this? Why did you buy it?"

"I don't remember," I told her, "but I read this book to Brett once in his car." I grabbed the book from her hand and threw it into the water. This time I watched it sink, the memory of that night drowning with it. "I know you probably think I'm being dramatic—"

"Stupid, actually."

"—but this makes me feel better. These books were safe. Like this alternate, paper world where anything was possible. And after my parents' divorce I gave up on love. I never wanted to fall into it or feel it because what was the point? These books let me feel it through other people. That way, I didn't have to worry about being hurt. It sounds dumb, but they helped. They helped me when nothing else could."

"So why throw them away?"

"Why do you care?" I asked, glancing up from the book in my lap to look at her. "We haven't really been friends for a long time."

Jenny shrugged, throwing another book in. "I know what it feels like to be alone. And that night, at the hotel, you looked like you could use someone to talk to. Not to mention I think you're having some sort of breakdown right now."

I ignored the last part. "Alone? You're never alone. You're always surrounded by your friends." I left out the night at the marsh.

Jenny had this sad smile on her face when she reached for another book. She held it in her lap, playing with the page corners. "You know," she said, "I used to think being popular was all that mattered. Having a lot of friends, being invited to parties, all of that shit. When I got my braces off before sophomore year and these"—she grabbed her chest—"finally grew in, people looked at me differently. Like I was now worthy of their attention or something. God, that sounds so superficial, and it was, but it felt really damn good. So I joined the cheerleading squad. I said yes when guys asked me on dates because what else was I supposed to do? I thought I was living this enviable life where everyone wanted to be me. And I was happy. But I was lonely, Becca. Because those people were my friends, but not like you once were."

She threw the book over the bridge.

"I'm sorry for ruining our friendship," she said. "I'm sorry for acting like I was better than you because I had more experience or whatever. You were a great friend. You still are. You deserved better than someone like me. But I'm happy that we're talking again. Think you can finally accept my two-year-late apology? Put the past behind us?"

I think the old me, the one in the hallway that day, would have said no. She would have happily accepted the answer to the question that had been weighing on her for years and gone on her way. She would have been fine losing another person because, after all, real life was scary and books were her only safe place. But I was starting to realize that maybe I wasn't that same girl anymore. So I said, "Yes," and hugged Jenny back when she reached out. Maybe with answers came forgiveness. And Jenny was the first person on that list.

When we were sitting side by side again, I said, "We were pretending," and, wow, it felt really good to say that out loud. "Me and Brett were never dating. It was all a lie."

Jenny laughed. She leaned back on the bridge, resting her palms flat behind her. "Honestly? I kind of thought the whole thing was bullshit," she said, shaking her curls out behind her. "Hand me one of those, would you?"

I reached into the bag blindly and gave her the first book my fingers touched. "You did? Why didn't you say anything? Tell anyone?"

She shrugged. "Who cares? Let people believe what they want. I think ninety percent of our school thinks I'm straight."

"You're not?"

She ripped the cover off the book in one swift motion. Making a face, she threw it into the water, then said, "Still figuring that out." Then she paused. "Let's keep that between us."

Obviously. "What about all those guys you dated?" I asked, curious.

"I don't know. Maybe I felt like I had to? Maybe that's why I was always bragging about it, to cover up something else I couldn't quite figure out yet. . . . You didn't answer my question. Why throw these books away?"

I thought about it for a moment. "Because they're fiction. They're not real. Love like this," I said, grabbing another book and waving it between us, "isn't real. It exists in these pages. That's it."

Then I had an idea. I grabbed the garbage bag, the whole thing, and stood up. I was about to throw it over the edge when Jenny screamed and ripped it out of my hands.

She placed it behind her, protecting it with her body, and muttering what sounded like "crazy" under her breath.

I was breathing hard. My fingers were tingling. I wanted to grab another book. I wanted to watch it drown.

I laughed again. This time, it was maniacal. Crazy. Total witch laugh.

"I can't believe it." I was shaking my head. "You were right this whole time! You told me these books were setting me up for disappointment, raising my expectations, and I didn't believe you. You were right," I said again.

I was still laughing when I lay back on the wood to stare up at the sky. Jenny's head appeared beside me a second later. I could feel her watching me, analyzing me like a puzzle. Like one right move and I could be put back together. I wasn't sure if I could. Because parts of myself were everywhere. Some with my mom, some with Cassie. Some were even with my dad. With Brett. And now, some were buried at the bottom of this lake, smudged words on soaked pages.

"What if," Jenny began slowly, "we were both wrong?" I raised my brows, shifted my head on the wood to stare at her. "I mean, these are books, Becca. They're not real life. You can't take what you read in here and expect it to magically happen to you. You can't expect it to feel like that."

She paused, grabbing a book out of the bag and placing it on her stomach. "Real guys aren't like this. I don't think anyone is like this. People don't stand in front of your bedroom window with a boom box—"

"That's from a movie. Not a book."

She gave me that look that said *shut up for a second.*

"My point is no one can live up to some romance you read about when you were fourteen. But Brett's *real.* He's here. And isn't that better? Mistakes and all?"

"Maybe," I said.

"He's been moping around school. Everyone knows what happened with his family. He's having a hard time. I'm sure he could use a friend. . . . Or a girlfriend."

"Fake girlfriend," I corrected her.

Jenny pushed my shoulder. "Please. Maybe it started off fake, but did it stay like that?" she asked.

I planted my elbow on the wood and raised myself up. "Give me the bag back," I said.

Slowly, Jenny handed it to me. "No more pollution?"

"No more pollution," I repeated.

"And you'll talk to Brett?" she prodded.

"To be determined."

"I want you to be happy, you know," Jenny said after a minute. Her eyes were still locked on the sky. "You seemed happy with him."

"I think I was."

"Give him time," she said. "Let him focus on his mom, his family. Once he gets that all sorted out, he'll come back."

"How do you know that?" I asked.

"Because some people leave for good. But sometimes they come back."

"Like you did," I said.

Jenny smiled. "Exactly."

I stood up then, bag in tow. It sagged in my hands, nearly empty now. I contemplated throwing it over, watching it sink, then decided against it. Maybe someday I'd pick up one of these books and be glad I didn't destroy it. Or maybe that day would never come and they'd just be books on a shelf. Either way, I walked off the bridge with the bag, Jenny trailing beside me.

The wind was picking up, blowing through the tree branches, and I smelled fried food. Like doughnuts. Why did the lake smell like doughnuts? Then I turned to Jenny and realized it was *her*. Then I realized my mom's bakery was just down the road, also the way Jenny came from . . .

"You were at my mom's bakery," I said.

"Those jelly things are addicting."

Brett

MY DAD WANTED TO GO to counseling. He thought a few hour-long sessions for our whole family would help us move past this, like his affair was nothing more than a bump in the road, a detour. That a few hours spent sitting on a couch talking to a stranger would magically fix this, then it would be back to his regularly scheduled family life.

My mind was made up and the answer was no. But my mom? My mom was all in.

The three of us were sitting on a couch in Dr. Kim's office. She kept taking down notes whenever my parents spoke. My dad was on his fifth "I'm sorry" and "It was a mistake" and my mom had already gone through two boxes off tissues. I hadn't said a word the entire session. The hour was almost up.

Dr. Kim turned to me. "You've been quiet, Brett," she said. "What's on your mind?"

"Nothing."

"You don't seem very happy to be here," she noted.

I looked at my mom, who'd finally stopped crying. The only reason I came was for her. I would have been fine changing all the locks on our house and not allowing my father back inside. But no, she wanted to try. And if that's what it took to make her happy, I'd do it.

"I'm not. I don't want to be here," I said, looking away from my mom. I picked up a stress ball off the table and squeezed it between my fingers.

"Why not?"

I let go, watched the ball return to normal size. "We're here to fix our family, right?"

She frowned. "Do you think your family is broken?"

"Yes," I said.

If Dr. Kim was annoyed with my short answers, she didn't show it. "And to use your word, do you want your family to be 'fixed'?" she asked.

I sank back into the couch, squeezing the ball harder until my knuckles started to turn white. "Yes."

217

Dr. Kim smiled, scribbling again in that notebook. "That's a good start. What do you think is the first step in making that happen?"

That was easy. "He has to leave."

My dad covered his head in his hands. My mom began to say my name before Dr. Kim cut her off. "That's okay, Willa. Let him finish. You think your dad leaving will fix your family, Brett?" she asked, turning back toward me.

"I think it would be a start," I said.

Satisfied, she wrote that down before turning to my father. "What do you think about that, Thomas?"

I had gotten into the habit of blocking out my dad's voice whenever he spoke. I focused on the stress ball and watched it expand and collapse. Then I looked around the room, at the dozens of plaques covering the walls. There were plants everywhere too, like someone had read a book on how to make a room feel welcoming. Too bad it wasn't working. All I wanted was to run out of there at full speed.

Finally, Dr. Kim closed her notebook. "Well, our time is up for today. But we can pick up from here next week." My parents shook her hand, said they'd schedule another appointment with the receptionist, and we left.

The hour-long drive home was silent. I didn't know if there were no family counselors in Crestmont or if my dad had just chosen one that was a few towns over. That way, it limited the chance someone would see us going. God forbid another Wells family secret was exposed.

No one said a single word the entire drive. The only sound was my mom sniffling and the low hum of the radio. The tension in the car was thick enough to make it hard to breathe. I opened a window and leaned my head outside, wishing this was a dream. It still didn't feel real. Any of this. I glanced at my dad's silhouette and then my mom's, then the space in the middle where their hands usually rested, intertwined, while driving. Now there was so much space between all three of us.

I could see my mom's face in the side-view mirror. Her head was resting against the window and her eyes were closed. She hadn't been sleeping lately. She spent all her time in her bedroom with the door half open, but she never slept. I started setting an alarm on my phone so I'd wake up in the middle of the night to check on her. Sometimes her bed was empty and I'd walk downstairs to find her sitting on the couch, staring at the TV screen. Most nights she was lying in bed crying. Those times, I'd lie beside her. She wouldn't say a word. She'd just hide the tissue box and hold my hand until the sun rose.

At this point I couldn't tell the difference between coping and surviving. There was no way our family could go back to normal. I was starting to forget what normal even felt like.

My dad dropped us off at home. I got out of the car and sat on the steps leading to the door. I watched him and my mom sit there for a few minutes, talking. They kept glancing at me. I was scared he'd get out and try to come inside, that he wouldn't want to go back to the hotel. But when the door opened, only my mom stepped out.

The house was so quiet. Eerie. I followed my mom into the kitchen and watched as she poured herself a mug of coffee. She looked skinnier. When was the last time she ate? I went to the fridge and started to make her a sandwich. That was my job now, to take care of her. She didn't say a word, just sat at the table and stared into the mug, not even drinking. When I placed the plate in front of her, she looked up at me. "What is this?"

"You need to eat, Mom."

She picked up half the sandwich and handed it to me, a silent offer. She'd only eat if I did too. Caving, I sat down and took a bite. Then she did.

We ate in silence.

"Your dad wants to come back home," my mom said.

I took a deep breath, swallowed down the anger. "Do you want that?" I asked.

She reached across the table, grabbed my hand. "I want what's best for you, Brett. That's all I ever wanted."

I read between the lines. "You could have told me, Mom, about the affair. You didn't have to go through that alone."

My mom patted my hand. Her face broke into this sad smile. "You love your father so much, Brett. I didn't want to take that away from you. And I'm your mother; it's my job to protect you."

"Do you still love him?"

"I do."

"Even after what he's done?" I asked.

"You can't shut off eighteen years of loving someone because of one mistake, Brett. Love is more complicated than that." My mom stood up, walked around the table, and hugged me from behind. She kissed my forehead, then walked away.

"Mom?" I called.

She paused at the doorway. "Yes?"

"Can I change the locks on the doors?"

"If you want."

I don't think it was that easy, though. Even if I physically removed my father from my life, he'd still be there. That was the worst part.

It was starting to feel like an earthquake had rocked through my life and split it into two. There was the mess waiting for me at home and then school, where I had to hide all the cracks. And now with Becca out of the picture, I wasn't sure which was worse.

It was my fault. I asked for space. And I wanted space, I really did. But I didn't realize that asking her to stop being my girlfriend also meant we couldn't be friends. In hindsight, I may have fucked that up. Because even though I was still trying to sift through my feelings, Becca was the only person I wanted to talk to. She was the only one who really understood. But from the looks of it, she wanted nothing to do with me. What I said that day on the rooftop had driven a wedge between us, because now she wouldn't even look at me. Not during class. Not during lunch. She even stopped eating at our table outside.

I tried to find her the first few days. I searched the library and the halls but she must have been hiding in some crevice only she knew about. The only time I got to see her was during English. On Thursday, our eyes met when Miss Copper asked me to stay back after class. And even then, Becca only held my gaze for a second before clutching her textbooks to her chest and rushing into the hall.

"Brett," Miss C said when the class had emptied. I stood before her desk, waiting. "I'm sure you are aware members of the football team need to maintain a B-grade in every class to continue playing."

I nodded. "I am."

She placed my recent essay on *Romeo and Juliet* on her desk. A big red F covered the top right corner. This week was turning into one bad moment after another. I wanted to explain why my paper was so bad. How I'd been so busy caring for my mom that I didn't have time to write it. That I was spending my weekend in some useless counseling session. How I was getting barely three hours of sleep a night because I wanted to stay awake in case the door opened and my dad tried to come home.

I just stood there, trying not to fall apart.

"This essay was worth thirty percent," she continued. "And with this low of a mark, your grade for this class has dropped to a C, Brett. I informed your coach and you'll have to start sitting out of football games until this changes."

"I'll bring my grade back up," I said. And this time it wasn't so I could play football for my dad. It was because I had an entire team relying on me.

"I trust that you will. And Brett?" Then she had that look on her face. The same pitiful one every other teacher was throwing me. Becca was right—the entire school knowing about my parents did suck. "If you need an extension in the future—"

"I won't. Thank you, Miss Copper," I said quickly before running out of class. I hated how everyone treated me like

I was broken, like they had to speak softer to make sure I wouldn't completely lose it. The only person treating me the same was Jeff, who was waiting in the hallway, eyes bugging out of his head.

"What happened?" he asked, following me to calculus.

"I failed that essay," I said, gripping the straps of my backpack. "My grade dropped to a C."

Jeff stopped walking. I kept walking until he tugged me backward. "You're off the team?"

"Would you keep your voice down?" I shoved him into the corner of the hall. "I'm not off the team. Just suspended until I bring my grade back up."

"So get a tutor. We need you on the team."

"There's a lot going on right now. I don't have time for a tutor."

He swore under his breath. "Right. I forgot. How's your mom doing?"

I shook my head. "She's a mess" was all I said. I didn't like talking about my family at school. "I have to get to class."

I made to turn around when his arm grabbed my shoulder. "Brett . . . are you okay?"

"I'm fine," I lied.

"You can tell me. We've been friends since we were kids." He took a step closer, lowering his voice. "I won't tell the team. It'll stay between us."

There were too many people in the halls, too many eyes on us. I didn't want to talk about this with him. Not now. Preferably not ever. The only person I wanted to confide in was Becca, and I'd lost that too.

"I'm fine," I repeated, pushing past Jeff and running down the stairs.

Maybe if I said it enough I could trick myself into believing it.

Becca

THE REVIVAL OF MY FRIENDSHIP with Jenny put a new spring in my step. It made me realize that ignoring Brett at school wasn't the way to deal with my problems. It was only going to widen the space that had opened up between us. I decided that it was time for me to take back the reins on my life and speak to Brett. He said he needed time to think, and a week was plenty of time, right? He had to have reached some conclusion on his feelings toward me. And whether good or bad, I was ready to find out. No more moping around for me. I had to take action.

So, on Monday morning, I walked into school with my head held high and one goal in mind.

Only Brett's seat in English class was empty.

All my determination and positive thinking was for nothing. Great.

I tried to pay attention to Miss Copper's lesson, but my eyes kept drifting to his desk, waiting for him to materialize out of thin air. My notes were suffering too. An hour had passed by and I had written one sentence. One!

During lunch, I ate at my usual table outside. Which, pathetically, felt a little lonelier without Brett there. I even had to throw half my fries out because he wasn't there to eat the rest. I was watching the doors, waiting for him to show up late. When the bell rang, I realized he wasn't just ghosting me. He was ghosting his entire education. And the thought made this knot grow in the pit of my stomach, because Brett wasn't the type to skip school. He'd only do that if he was desperate. Like if things had gotten worse at home.

I should have called him to check in. We were kind of allies in the broken-family department. And allies don't abandon each other.

After school, I plopped myself down on the grass beneath the oak tree and waited for football practice to start. The doors to the locker room opened and the players trickled out. I watched, waiting to see Brett and that head of golden hair. Jeff was out first, then a bunch of other players whose names I didn't know and who I had never spoken to. The door shut, the coach blew his whistle, and they all huddled in the center of the field.

I took out my book and read a page, waiting. Maybe Brett was running late.

I read a chapter. Still waiting. He had to show up. He specifically said he wasn't going to quit the team.

I read until one hour had passed. Their shirts were off now, and they were all lying on their backs in the grass, splashing water on their faces. Brett was nowhere to be found.

I picked up my book and my bag and walked down the hill, across the field, and toward the metal bench that Jeff was sitting on. "Hey, Jeff," I said. His eyes squinted in the sun when they met mine. "Have you seen Brett?"

He set his phone aside. "You don't know?"

Oh god. The knot in my stomach doubled. "Know what?"

"He's off the team." My mouth literally dropped open like a puppet. "Not permanently," he added quickly. "Just till he brings his grade up. This happened a few days ago. . . . He hasn't told you?"

Clearly Brett hadn't filled his best friend in on our breakup.

"We haven't spoken in a while" was all I said.

228

"Last I heard he was looking for someone to tutor him in English."

"He's failing English?" My heart dropped. That was my best subject and he didn't ask for my help? *Of course he didn't*, a voice in my head said. *You've been hiding from him for a week.* Shut up shut up shut up.

"How has he been?" I asked then, lowering my voice. "With his family."

Jeff kicked stubbornly at the grass. "I don't know. He won't talk to me about it."

But I knew he'd talk to me.

"You think he's home right now?" I checked my phone for the time. "I can walk there in twenty minutes if I take the side roads," I said, thinking out loud.

"I can give you a ride," Jeff said, nodding toward the field. "We're almost done here. Mind waiting fifteen?"

I told him that no, I didn't, then made a beeline inside. With half the contents of my locker piled into my backpack and my arms, I sat on the front steps and waited. Twenty minutes had passed when Jeff showed up. "This way," he said, leading me to an old red pickup truck that was equal parts car and rust. It looked like it was going to crumble apart at any moment. Suddenly, walking to Brett's house felt like a better option.

"The car's fine," Jeff said, reading my mind. "I got the brakes fixed last week." How reassuring. I sat down anyway. Desperate times and all that.

"You've met Brett's parents?" I asked when we were driving through town.

"Loads of times."

"What do you think of them?"

"Before all of this happened? I thought they were cool, like any normal parents. Always holding hands, coming to the football games together, that kind of stuff. I never would have guessed that his dad . . . I don't think anyone saw that coming. Especially Brett. The guy practically worshipped his dad."

"He hasn't said anything to you about his family?" I asked again.

"Brett's private, I guess. I tell him he can talk to me about this stuff but he won't. At this point I just figured if he wants to talk, he will. I won't push him. We're here."

I nearly flew out of the car before we were even parked. "Thanks for the ride," I said, then ran up the driveway. I knocked once. Took a deep breath in. Blew it out. Knocked again. I was beginning to think no one was home when the door pulled open and Brett was there, standing in front of me, staring into my eyes in that way that made my fingers shake. My first thought was, *Wow, he looks different.*

Stubble lined his jaw, and he looked like he had just rolled out of bed. His eyes went from my face to the hoard of textbooks in my hands.

"Becca." He said my name slowly. "What are you doing here?"

"You're failing English," I said.

His eyebrows scrunched together. "How do you know that?" Then he spotted Jeff's pickup in the driveway and put the pieces together. "Of course he told you."

I had to remind myself he was going through a lot right now. Yelling out of frustration would not make this any better. "*You* should have told me," I said, trying to sound as calm as possible. "I know you said you needed space, Brett, but this seems like the kind of emergency that takes priority over that."

"It was one essay. I'm working on rewriting it."

"Do you want some help?" I asked. I was shifting on my feet, waiting for him to say no, shut the door, and go back to his separate little world.

He opened the door farther. "Sure."

I headed straight to Brett's kitchen and slammed my textbooks down onto the table. I took out my notebooks and pens and rearranged them into a neat little row. "Grab your essay," I called, assuming he was listening, "and bring it here so I can read it over and see what needs to be fixed."

I waited to hear footsteps or some sign of movement. There was nothing. I turned around. He was standing in the doorway, watching me. "Brett? What is it?"

He shook his head. "Nothing."

"Then would you sit your ass down so we can get started, please?"

"Did you just say ass?"

"Sit down."

He held his hands up in surrender and took a seat. Sliding his laptop across the table, Brett pulled up his essay and let me read it. I could understand why Miss Copper gave him an F. It was terrible. The ideas were all over the place and the quotes weren't even properly cited.

I looked up at him. "How long did it take you to write this?"

He thought about it for a second. "An hour?"

"It shows. This makes zero sense, Brett. You don't even have a thesis."

He shifted in his seat, drew up the hood of his sweater until it covered half his face. "I kind of forgot it was due. And I was up all night with my mom so I didn't have time to write it."

Then I felt like a complete jerk. "Right, of course. Sorry. Forget I said that." I kept scrolling through the essay, noticing how Brett was really quiet. I snuck a peek at him.

He was staring at his hands on the table. I shut the laptop and pushed it aside. "We don't need to study right now," I said. "We can talk about your family if you want."

Brett lifted his eyes to mine. "I'd actually rather study," he said.

So we did. I printed out Brett's essay and we went through it line by line. I started to highlight the parts he needed to change and suddenly three-quarters of the pages were yellow. We came up with a new thesis, found good quotes, and outlined his arguments. An hour later he had rewritten the introduction while I watched over his shoulder. I could tell he was starting to get antsy; he was writing slower and slower. His attention kept slipping and eventually he opened a new browser tab for a pizza place nearby.

"I'm starving," he declared. "You in?"

We spent the next ten minutes concocting the perfect pizza. Brett was a meat-lover's kind of guy, which, for some reason, was not all that surprising. All I cared about was pineapple being on it.

"Do we want garlic sticks?" he asked. I gave him a what-kind-of-insane-question-is-that look. He changed the quantity to two.

After the order was placed, we went back to studying. I was flipping through my English notebook absent-mindedly while Brett continued typing out his essay. Then something caught my eye. There were numbers written on the back cover. It was my countdown to graduation. Only I had stopped counting one day without realizing it. When did I stop keeping track?

Brett slid the laptop over to me. "Does this make sense?" he asked.

He was the answer, the reason I stopped counting the days. Brett gave me something better to look forward to.

"Why are you smiling at me like that?"

I cleared my throat, quickly shoved the notebook into my bag. "What? Nothing. Let me see." I scanned the paragraph and told him that yes, it made sense.

We kept working in silence for another few minutes before Brett's mind was officially elsewhere. He had deleted and retyped the same sentence five times. Thankfully the doorbell rang, the pizza arrived, and we both took a break. I chewed on a slice, watching suspiciously as Brett picked off all the pineapple pieces.

"If you don't like pineapple, why agree to order it?" I asked.

"Because you like it," he said easily.

"You wouldn't eat the cotton candy ice cream," I pointed out.

"That happens to be where I draw the line, Becca."

"Right."

The smallest of smiles began to crack through his unnaturally stony face.

"I'm wondering," he said, grabbing another slice, "where you've been eating lunch this past week. I looked around the entire school and couldn't find you."

I narrowed my eyes. "You were looking for me?"

"I was."

"But you said you wanted space."

"That," he said, taking another bite, "was a mistake. Coincidentally, you happen to be the one person I don't want space from. So, where were you eating?"

I forced myself to swallow. "Behind the football field."

He raised his eyebrows. "You walked that far to get away from me?"

"As I said, *you* wanted space. Not me. I was simply obliging."

"Do me a favor, Hart. Next time I tell you I want space, ignore me."

"Noted."

Brett stood up and walked to the fridge. "Hey, where's your mom?" I asked.

"She's staying with my aunt for the night," he said, walking back with two water bottles.

"And your dad?" I asked slowly, not wanting to push too hard.

"He's been staying at a hotel for the week." Brett sat back down, this time in the chair directly beside me, and handed me one of the bottles. "We've been going to family counseling."

"Wow. What was that like?"

"Other than a waste of two hundred dollars? Pointless. My mom cries the whole time. My dad talks about how sorry he is. But it doesn't count if he's only sorry *after* he got caught." Brett paused, drank half the water bottle. "I sit there and wait for the hour to pass by."

I grabbed the last corner slice of pizza. "My mom never tried the therapy route. I did see her reading one of those self-help books once. It was called *Children and Divorce* or something like that."

"And? Did it work?"

"Apparently the bookworm trait is not genetic. She turned to baking instead. But we got jelly bells out of it, so not complaining."

Brett's face took on this dreamy look, like he too was thinking about those magnificent doughnuts. I should have brought him some. It would have been a way better ice-breaker than me shoving textbooks in his face. Speaking of his face, it was so close. And his eyes were kind of hypnotic. I always thought I liked his smile the most. But his eyes were something else.

"You're staring at me."

"I'm looking at your eyes," I said quickly. "Before I knew you, that was the one thing girls always talked about. Your eyes."

He looked genuinely surprised. "My *eyes*? Not my amazing football talents or hot bod?"

I stifled a laugh. "Nope. Just the eyes."

"Well, tell me, Becca. What do they say about my eyes?"

"That they're nice. Dreamy. *Swoon-worthy.*"

"Do they?" he said, wiggling his eyebrows. "And what do you think about my eyes?"

I swallowed this weird lump that rose in my throat and said, "Your eyes are nice. They're like the ocean. Calm."

"Oceans can be deadly."

I was starting to think Brett was too. Or at least the way he made me feel was. Like I was standing on the edge of a cliff. Or riding a roller coaster that only went up.

"Hey," he said suddenly, "do you wanna get out of here?"

"But we have to finish your essay."

"We can finish it later. This will only take an hour."

It was kind of ridiculous that he expected me to say no.

It had been so long since I'd seen him like this, somewhat happy, that I would have said yes to anything just to make him stay like that a little longer.

So when Brett held out his hand, I took it.

We ended up at Finch's, the only bookstore in town. Brett paused in front of the door and spread his arms out like *ta-da!*, with this larger-than-life smile on his face.

"You . . . brought me to a bookstore?" I asked, looking between him and the doors, not really catching on. "Do you need another book for your essay?"

"Noooo," he said, stretching the word out and taking a step closer. "I thought I should repay you, Becca. You helped me study, you came to my football games and to the arcade. We've done so many things for me. It's time we do something that you like. Don't you think?"

I mean, I couldn't argue with that.

And I wanted to go inside. Badly.

"I'm having trouble deciding whether or not you like this," Brett said.

I couldn't help it anymore. I threw my arms around him and pressed my face to his chest. "I love it, Brett. Thank you." And what I loved the most was how the space that had opened up between us seemed to be almost entirely gone.

We stood there for a second before Brett said, "You're dying to go inside and run through the aisles. Aren't you?"

"Very much. Yes."

He held open the door and gave me a little nudge. "Go crazy."

I ran inside. The store was empty aside from Mr. Finch, who was standing behind the counter, half asleep. He gave me a little wave—I was a regular here, to say the least—and then I set off for the aisles with Brett hot on my trail. We spent an hour huddled between rows and rows of books. It was dreamy, really. Totally swoon-worthy, sort of like Brett's eyes. I read the summary of every book aloud, waiting for his approval. If he nodded, I added it to our bag. If he scrunched his nose up (which he usually did) I put it back on the shelf before trying another.

Apparently Brett was very picky. More so than me. I couldn't be too picky now. I needed new books to read after the mass paper-murder I committed on the bridge. Which, looking back, may have been a smidge uncalled for.

"What's the last book you read?" I asked Brett.

He plucked a book off the shelf, rolled his eyes, then placed it back. "*Romeo and Juliet*," he said.

"We were forced to read that for class, Brett."

"So? Still counts."

It definitely did not!

I walked over to the counter with a total of four books in my bag. "How long will it take you to read all these? A few weeks? A month?" Brett asked while Mr. Finch scanned everything.

I scoffed. He had so much to learn. "Try a week."

"Thirty-five dollars and twenty-one cents," Mr. Finch said.

I started reaching for my wallet when Brett stopped me. "I got this," he said. "My treat. Remember?"

"Thank you."

He just smiled, saying nothing while kind of saying everything.

When we walked outside, I headed toward the car but Brett grabbed my hand, pulling me over to a bench on the side of the street. He sat down and tapped the empty spot beside him. I took a seat, placing the book bag in my lap. It was a little cold out now that the sun had set and the wind picked up. It was blowing my hair around my shoulders, fanning it into my face while I scrambled to pull it back. Brett laughed beside me and the sound seemed to carry into the air, playing like a symphony being strummed by the stars.

"You're wearing the ring," Brett said, startling me.

"What? Oh." I held up my hand, staring at the rose ring on my finger. It was the prize we won at the arcade. "I like it," I said.

There were many things I liked. Many of those I wanted to share with Brett. With the quiet settling around us, I could have. But now that we were together again, it was like all the words my mind had planned out were gone. And all I really wanted was to kiss him. This time, I didn't want it to be fake. I wanted it to be as real as this moment felt.

The scariest part was, I still didn't know if this was real to him.

I jumped when Brett tapped his finger against my forehead. He was watching me, smiling. "What's on your mind?" he asked.

"I was thinking about what you said that night at the hotel. That you couldn't decide if what you felt for me was real."

The memory still felt a little raw. From the way Brett winced at the mention of it, it was like that for him too. But we had spent a week avoiding each other and dodging the subject. Normally, that would be fine with me. After all, I was a master in burying my emotions. But there was something about Brett that made me want to grab a shovel and dig them all up. Everything I felt for him was good and light and warm. Not dark like I was used to. Why would I want to ignore that?

"I was wondering," I continued, "if you figured that out yet. . . ."

"Oh," he said. "That."

"Yeah. That."

Then Brett scooted across the bench, moved a little closer. It was only an inch or so, but enough for my heart to start playing Ping-Pong against my rib cage.

"I've been thinking about that night a lot," he said.

"So have I."

"And what I realized," Brett continued, "is that nothing I felt toward you was tainted or confusing, Becca. In fact, you're the only clear part of my life right now."

He moved a little closer.

I moved a little closer too.

"You know what I like about you?" he said.

I tried to hide my smile but I could feel it breaking across my face. "What?"

"I like how you have the absolute worst taste in food," he said, moving another inch across the bench.

"Agree to disagree," I chimed in.

"I like how you don't even flinch when we watch scary movies," Brett continued. Paused. Moved a little closer. "I like how you always get lost in thought, like you live half your life inside your head. And I like how your face turns all pink whenever you catch me staring at you." As if on cue, my face started to heat up. "See?"

There was no space between us on the bench now.

We were thigh to thigh. Knee to knee. I was all warm and tongue-tied. My brain went to mush whenever Brett was this close.

"Sooooo," I said, inching my hand closer to his. "What does all that mean?"

"It means," Brett said, wrapping his pinky around mine, "that I like you. A lot. And that I was a jerk to ever doubt that. A lot of things have been changing in my life, Becca. In this whole mess, you're the only constant. You're the one that always comes back."

"I'm still a little unclear on what you mean," I said, smiling.

Brett gave me a look. "Is this some sort of payback?"

"Maybe."

"Fine." I shrieked as he reached out and grabbed my waist, pulling me across the bench until I was halfway on his lap. My first reaction was to make sure no one was lingering on the street, watching. They weren't. Then I let myself relax, grabbed Brett's face in my hands.

"Can we give this one more shot?" he said. "No more pretending. No more space. No more people coming between us. One last try. I won't mess it up this time."

"Only real from here on out?" I asked.

Brett smiled, pressed his check into my palm. "Only real."

He leaned in, touched his mouth to mine ever so lightly.

It was nowhere near enough.

"One more question," I said. He made a very agitated noise in response. "Our first kiss in the hallway, rate it on a scale of one to ten."

Brett pulled his face back a little. "Are you being serious?"

"Yes. Rate it."

"A nine. Why?"

I shrugged. "I thought it was only me that felt that. I mean, it was my first kiss, so I didn't have much to compare it to. But it's nice to know you thought so too."

"That was your first kiss?" I nodded. "Tell me, Becca," Brett said, running his thumb across my bottom lip. "If this were a book, how'd you want your first kiss to be?"

"I don't know," I said honestly. I never really thought about that.

"Come oooon. I don't believe that for a second. Would it be raining? What about fireworks? Or would it be late at night when you're sitting on a bench in front of a bookstore?"

"That doesn't sound *totally* horrible," I said.

Brett took my face in his hands then, gently. He moved closer until I could see nothing but those deadly ocean eyes. "I think you're amazing," he said, "and I think you deserve a first kiss that's a hell of a lot better than standing in a school hallway while everyone watches."

"Like sitting on a bench with no one watching?"

"Becca," he said, closing the space between us until our foreheads were touching, "your first kiss should have been like this."

I wondered if Brett could feel how quickly my heart was beating when his mouth touched mine, or if he could feel the shift too. Because in that moment, something changed. Like the world remolded itself around the two of us.

I didn't question why my heart was burning when I wrapped my arms around his neck or why it felt like it would fall out of my chest. I only pulled him closer until we were one silhouette of lips and hands and beating hearts against the night sky.

I wasn't sure who pulled away first. All I knew was that it was too soon, and my heart no longer felt like it was entirely mine. It was shared somewhere between the both of us.

"That," Brett whispered, "was an eleven."

I was thinking more of a twelve.

Brett

IT HAD TO BE IN here somewhere.

I was rummaging through my closet, trying to find my black denim jacket to wear tonight. There was a new horror movie playing in town and, in light of Becca's obsession with all things scary, I told her I'd take her. Only the film started in a little over an hour and I couldn't find my damn jacket.

I was pulling boxes off shelves and throwing them onto the floor. There were hangers everywhere like my room had turned into an out-of-control garage sale. I was digging through boxes on the top shelf, knowing full well my jacket would not be there, when I found a blue box. Seeing it kind of knocked the air from my lungs. I held it in my hands and sank down on my bed.

Slowly, I took the lid off.

Everything was in there. The first football my dad ever bought me. Polaroid photos of the two of us at my football games as a kid. My old cleats, jerseys, trophies. It was a box of memories I'd forgotten I even had.

My mom came running into my room. "Brett! What was that— What happened in here?"

I couldn't take my eyes off the box. I picked up a photo. My dad and I were smiling at the camera. I was missing my two front teeth and my hair was long, covering both my eyes. I think I was nine or ten when this was taken. I could still smell the grass and feel my dad's arm on my shoulder. He looked so happy. So proud. We both did.

My mom sat beside me on the bed, placed her hand on mine.

"I always loved that photo," she said. "You know, your dad still talks about that day all the time. It was one of his favorites."

"Mine too."

"He was so proud of you, Brett. He still is."

I put the picture back in the box and picked up another. My mom was in this one. It was sophomore year, after I made the football team at school. It was my first game and my parents had come to watch. They sat in the bleachers, and I remembered how I could hear my dad's voice yelling over the entire crowd. We took that photo after we had won the game. It was on the desk in my dad's office until he replaced it with a new one. I kept it here, locked in this box.

My mom rested her head on my shoulder. I knew she was remembering that day too. It felt like a different life, a different timeline where everything was similar and different at once. And for the first time, this tiny, small part of me missed my dad. Missed that weight of his arm on my shoulder.

"Mom? Can I ask you something?" She was sorting through the box, unknotting the laces on my old cleats. "If you didn't have to worry about me, what would you do about Dad?"

"What do you mean?"

"You said you were trying to protect me. Right? That's why you didn't tell me Dad was having an affair. But what if you didn't have me to worry about? Then what would you do? Would you stay with him? Divorce him? How would you protect yourself?"

She let out a long, tired breath and moved back on my bed until she was sitting against the headboard. She patted the empty spot beside her and I lay down on my back, still clutching that photo between my fingers, that reminder of a different time.

"I think . . . ," she began, looking up at the ceiling, "I wouldn't get a divorce. I would stay with him."

"Why?"

"Because I love him." She said it so easily. "Because I believe him when he says he's sorry."

"But how do you know he really means it?" I asked.

"Because he's trying, Brett. He's really trying with these counseling sessions. He wants to make everything okay. Look around you—at this house, this life. He's spent all these years working so hard so we could have this. I've loved your father since I was seventeen years old, and in all those years, this is the one big mistake he's made. How do we decide if one mistake is worth giving all of this up? The life we've built together?"

My mom sat up, placed her hand on my shoulder. I looked her in the eye and I could see it, how much she loved him. How much she wanted to be with him. And all this time I thought this past week was only hard on her because the truth was out. But maybe I was wrong. Maybe it was hard because my dad was staying at the hotel and she was away from the person she loved. And I had made that decision for her out of anger. I took my mom's choice away because I thought I was protecting her, when really I was only thinking about myself.

"Mom?" I said, holding both her hands in mine. "All I want is for you to be happy. That's it. And if our family staying the same makes you happy, then . . ." I took a deep breath, forced the words out. "I'm okay with that. I'll go to counseling. I'll try with Dad. I'll try for *you*. But if you decide that you want everything to change, to get a divorce and never look back, then that's okay too. I want whatever's best for you because that'll be what's best for me too. Okay?"

I was so used to seeing my mom cry that when the tears started to spill, I didn't even flinch. And I realized that all I really wanted was for her to not cry anymore. If that meant sitting in an office with Dr. Kim and talking about my feelings or opening the door and letting my dad back inside—I'd do that for her.

I hugged my mom, held her so close to my chest and wished I could make this all okay.

"He's not a terrible dad, Brett," she said. "If he was, you wouldn't have ended up like this, with a heart as big as yours."

Then she took one last look at the photo and walked away.

I was lifting my hand to knock a second time on Becca's door when it opened. She took one look at me and her eyes went wide. "Oh no," she breathed. The door opened a little more and I could see her fully. Messy hair and unicorn pajamas. Not exactly movie attire.

"You forgot," I said.

"I'm *so* sorry, Brett. Oh my gosh. I was helping my mom out with this new recipe and I totally lost track of time. I'm sorry. Come in, I'll get dressed and we can leave. The trailers usually take forever, right? So we won't miss that much of the movie. Maybe only the opening credits or the first few minutes. . . ."

"Becca."

"What?"

I pushed open the door, stepped inside, and pulled her to me. "You're talking very fast," I said.

She began to smile. "I do that sometimes. Sorry I forgot."

"It's okay."

She pulled my face down to hers. She smelled like vanilla. Tasted like it too. Then her mom walked into the hallway and Becca jumped away from me like she'd been electrocuted.

"Brett, you're here! I was just saying how we could use another set of hands for this recipe. Want an apron?"

I grinned. "I would love one."

"Mom," Becca groaned. "We're going to watch a movie."

"No, that's okay. We can skip it and help," I said. Clearly

not the right answer because Becca looked absolutely mortified as we walked into the kitchen. I swear I heard her whisper my name and "fiasco" under her breath.

"Wonderful! We were just reminiscing about that time I bought Becca an Easy-Bake Oven and she almost lit the kitchen on fire."

"Oh, I would *love* to hear that story, Ms. Hart."

She handed me a bowl and a whisk at the same time as Becca reached out and smacked my shoulder. "This is not okay," she hissed while her mom went on with the story.

"Nice pajamas," I whispered back.

I had never seen her look so angry.

"So what are we making?" I asked, shrugging off my jacket and placing it over the chair. The counter was covered with baking sheets, cupcake trays, and some circle pan thing with a hole in the middle.

"That's a Bundt," Becca said, following my gaze.

"I knew that."

She stuck her tongue out.

"We're making," her mother began, pressing some buttons on the stove, "a new recipe that is either going to be some sort of cake, sheet cake, or cupcake."

"My mom is convinced she can make lemon and chocolate taste good together," Becca explained.

"It will taste great, and it will definitely give jelly bells a run for their money."

"I'm not sure that's possible," Becca added.

"I'm with Becca on that one," I said.

Her mom pointed a batter-covered spoon at us. "You two wait and see. I have an eye for bringing together unnatural pairings."

Becca

JENNY SHOWED UP AT MY locker after last period.

"I was thinking of swinging by the bakery and getting a dozen of those jelly bells. You in?" she asked.

I still wasn't entirely used to the two of us being friends again. It felt like I'd been swept into a wormhole and dropped off in another dimension. Or I'd traveled back in time to freshman year.

I shut my locker, pulled my bag onto my shoulder. "You're inviting me to my own mother's business?"

"Is that a yes or no?"

"Yes, obviously."

We left school together. Walking beside Jenny was the same as walking beside Brett. We couldn't make it down one hall without at least three different people trying to talk to her. Eventually we escaped, and while we walked down the road to Main Street, Jenny was staring down at her phone.

"Everything okay?"

She looked up. "My brother's girlfriend broke up with him a few days ago," she explained. "His social media has been taken over by all these sappy quotes about love he keeps posting."

"Why'd they break up?"

"He won't tell me. Or anyone. My parents don't even know about it."

"You never really talked about him," I said, referencing the time we used to be friends. Which, now, didn't feel so long ago.

"Parker's in college now, he's two years older than us. He's my parents' pride and joy. They've been training him to take over the family business since he was in diapers. He practically sucks all the attention out of every room we're in." She must have noticed the way I was looking at her, because she added, "This is not a pity party or anything. I'm not some neglected daughter. I actually like all the attention being on him. Lets me do whatever I want without my parents noticing. What about you? What are your plans after we graduate and leave this dump?"

"No idea," I said honestly.

"Same. My parents don't like that. They want to map out my future like they did for Park. But I kind of like not having a destination in mind. It's like whatever happens, happens. As long as it's not in Crestmont," she added, bumping her shoulder against mine.

"Agreed."

When we walked into the bakery, my mom was standing behind the counter, handing a box to a customer. The place was busier than usual. Almost all the tables were full and there was an actual line that started at the counter and went halfway through the store.

My mom's face lit up when she spotted the two of us. "Becca!" she called, waving her hands over her head like she was guiding an airplane for landing.

I went to the front of the line, ignoring the dirty looks from one woman who thought I was cutting in. "Why is it so busy? Did those flyers catch on?"

"I wish. A bus broke down off the highway," she explained. "Long story, but now all of these people are stuck here. And they're starving. Can you handle the cash register? I need to help Cassandra in the back."

I looked at the line of customers waiting. My mom was right. They looked exhausted and hungry, like they'd jump over the counter any second.

"Becca?" my mom asked again, holding out her apron.

"I'll cover cash. Go help in the back."

"I can help too," Jenny added.

My mom looked like she was about to hug her. "Stay here with Becca and help with the line," she said before running off into the back. I quickly put the apron on and got set up behind the counter.

I turned to Jenny, handed her a spare apron. "I'll take the orders, you prepare them. There's tongs and boxes behind you. Good?"

She nodded. We faced the line together.

"Next!" I called.

An hour later the line was gone, there were empty cupcake wrappers littering the floor, and half the tables were either missing a chair or had too many extra ones. Cassie was sitting down in one, looking like she'd just run a marathon. We all looked that way.

The door to the bakery opened and we all groaned.

"Welcome to—" I began before Jenny cut me off.

"That's my brother," she said, taking off her apron and hanging it on the hook on the wall. I looked at the guy standing in the doorway—curly black hair, dark skin, dressed in slacks and a button-up. He looked different than my vague memory of him.

"Thank you for your help, Jennifer," my mom said, giving her a quick hug.

"Anytime, Ms. Hart. I'll see you at school, Becca." She walked over to her brother and the two of them left without another word.

"*That's* Parker?" Cassie gawked, pressing her face into the window and watching them leave. "He looks so different from high school."

The bell chimed again a few minutes later. A family walked in with two children. I took their order, handed them their food, and they took a seat at the table beside the window.

I watched them eat. The kids had strawberry jelly smeared all over their faces and their mother kept leaning across the table with a napkin to wipe it off. The dad was sitting back in his chair, watching the three of them with a smile on his face. The sugar-packet tower the little boy built tipped over and he started to cry. The mom closed her eyes, like she really needed a break from crying, before her husband reached across the table and started to rebuild the tower. The little boy stopped crying.

It was all so normal. Taking your children to a bakery in town and building towers out of sugar. And even though one of them looked exhausted and the other was crying, the controlled sense of chaos was wrapped in a thin veil of love.

I looked at Cassie, sweeping the floors with half her hair sticking out from her ponytail.

I turned to the window into the back room and saw my mom kneading dough at the counter, flour on her cheeks. She glanced up, spotted me, and smiled.

I looked back at the family and realized not everything had to be conventional. Life didn't have to fit into a four-sided box that was neat and tidy. It was okay if the box had three sides or the fourth one was hanging on with duct tape. It was okay if the corners were dented and if there was a big red FRAGILE sticker on top.

It was all okay.

I took off my apron and placed it on the counter. "Mom," I called, running into the back. "Can you and Cass close tonight? I have something I need to do."

She looked up from the dough. "Of course. Where are you—"

"Thanks!"

There was all this anticipation building up inside me. I felt great. Grand. Energized. Larger than life. I grabbed my coat and ran out the front door before Cassie even looked up from the broom. I was running down the street, my feet following that familiar path they'd walked in secret for too long now. Not anymore. There were no more secrets. After today, there'd be no more FRAGILE sticker on this box.

I ran past the bookstore. Past the church. Past the intersection that led home. I ran and ran and ran until I was standing on his street. I hunched over, hands on my knees, caught my breath, then ran again. I had to keep moving. If I stopped to think, I might turn back around and let another five years pass by. Not anymore. I was tired of having one foot stuck in the past when I was trying to move into the future.

I had let myself fall for Brett. I didn't hide those feelings down inside me anymore. I shoveled them up and brought them into the light. But there was still a little darkness buried in some corner within me. There were still questions lingering that I had been too scared to say out loud.

I wasn't scared anymore.

I ran to my dad's house, up the driveway, and knocked on the door. My heart was beating too fast. Unnaturally fast. I couldn't breathe and I couldn't think and then the door was opening and his wife was standing there. There was a baby girl squirming around in her arms.

"Becca," she said. "You're back."

She knew who I was. All this time.

"Is my dad home?" I asked.

"I'm Maeve," she said, holding out her hand. "It's nice to officially meet you."

"My dad—"

"Is probably in his office, nose stuck in a book. I'll go get him."

I felt sick, nauseated as she walked down the hall. I told my brain to ignore the book comment but it was all I could focus on. It was so weird that there was this person, this huge part of who I was, living a few streets down from me. He'd felt so far away all these years when he was right here, reading and laughing and having children and starting over.

I almost turned around. I almost ran back down the driveway, but I couldn't run forever. I had to do this. For myself and for my mom. For Brett. For us. For the future I wanted to have and the person I wanted to be in it.

Footsteps from down the hallway pulled me back to the door, to the person now walking toward me. I had seen him from afar all those days I watched from down the street. But this—this was different. This was real. There were no more separate lives. It was a full-blown collision.

Now I could see the gray strands of hair interspersed with the brown. I could see the lines wrinkling the corners of his eyes and the hand with that shiny new wedding band. I had never met such a familiar stranger.

"Becca." His voice took me back to every memory, every moment. "I can't believe you're here," he said, holding his arms out to hug me. "I've missed you."

I didn't move.

His arms dropped to his sides.

"I live close by," I said quietly.

His eyebrows crinkled together. It made him look older. "What?"

I cleared my throat. "I live a few streets away. If you really missed me that much, you could have tried to visit."

His face fell. "You're right. I'm sorry." Then he smiled and said, "You're so grown up. You look just like your mother."

And that was it. Five years of being absent had led to an uncomfortable conversation between two people who no longer knew each other.

All I wanted was to be around my real family now. Around my mom and Brett. Around Cassie. Around the people who had never let me down.

"I'm not here to repair our relationship. I don't want you in my life, Dad." The word slipped out before I could stop it. It felt wrong because "dad" wasn't just a title. There was so much meaning behind it. Meaning that no longer applied to him.

I thought it was impossible for him to look any sadder than he did right then. "I don't understand. Then why are you here?" he asked.

I took a deep breath and then I said the words that had been stuck somewhere between my heart and my head for far too long. "I'm here to forgive you. I spent the last five years living with this weight inside of me. A weight that's there because of you. I tried to forget you. I tried to press the thought of you down until you were nothing but a distant memory and for a while, I thought it worked. . . . But now I'm falling in love. And that made me realize just how much damage you did to my heart.

"I can't live with this pain anymore. I can't carry around this sadness because it's stopping me from being the person I want to be. I . . . I can't be that person if I still hate you." I whispered the last part. Even after everything, it still broke my heart to say these words that would break his. "I forgive you for leaving us."

"I'm not sure I deserve your forgiveness," he whispered.

"You don't. But I'm giving it to you anyway."

We were silent for a moment. I realized it had begun to rain. It was a drizzle, a few drops landing on my shoulders. Not loud enough to hear, but faint enough that you couldn't ignore it either.

"You're falling in love?" he asked.

"I am," I said, wiping a tear off my cheek, "and it's greater than any book I ever read."

Suddenly, I wanted to continue. I wanted to tell my father all about Brett and the way he made me feel. I wanted him to know everything and my heart burned for the man I used to look up to. But I had to remind myself that man was gone. The person standing in front of me was not the father I had known five years ago, and he had lost the right to know about my life the night he walked out the door.

I began to walk away, back down the steps, and then I stopped. There was one last question I needed an answer to. "Was it worth it?" I asked, turning around. "Leaving us for this new life. Was it worth it? Are you happier?"

"I don't know how to respond to that," he said.

That was all the answer I needed.

"Goodbye, Dad."

The walk down the driveway felt like miles. It was raining now, pouring down and soaking through my clothes. I stopped, turned my face to the sky, and let the water wash the past off me. The memories and the pain and all those questions that had held me down like an anchor—I stood there and smiled as they washed away. And for the first time in years, it felt like that constant weight pressing down on my chest was gone. I could breathe freely.

I started to run then, down another familiar route. This time I ended up at Brett's house. I was soaking wet when I knocked on the door and I couldn't stop smiling. I felt so happy. So normal.

When Brett pulled open the door, I jumped into his arms. I grabbed his face and I kissed him because now I wanted to move into the future with him.

I was laughing when our faces parted. "Hi," I said.

He was smiling, sun after a rainstorm.

"Hi," he said back. Then we both realized it was still raining and the door was wide open. Brett pulled me inside. "Let me get you a towel." He disappeared down the hall and jogged back, towel in hand. He wrapped it around my shoulders, rubbed his hands up and down my arms.

"Brett!" a voice called from the other room. His mom. "Who's here?"

"Becca!" Brett yelled back. Then he turned toward me. "You wanna watch a movie with us?"

I told him yes, there was actually nothing I'd like more than that.

We walked into the living room and his mom was sitting on the couch, wrapped up in a blanket. The television was paused but I was staring at the man sitting beside her. It was Brett's father. I quickly glanced at Brett, studying his face for some hidden trace of anger. But he was smiling, and he seemed genuinely . . . okay.

"Dad," he said, slipping his arm around my waist, "this is my girlfriend, Becca."

I shook his hand in a daze. "It's a pleasure to finally meet you," he said. He had the exact same eyes as Brett.

"You too, Mr. Wells."

I sat next to Brett on the couch. His mother clicked play

on the remote and the movie began. Minutes had passed before I turned to him and whispered, "Brett?"

He tilted his head toward mine. "Yes?"

I looked at his parents, then back to him. "Is this okay?" I whispered.

He nodded, squeezed my hand. With the smallest of smiles, he said, "I think so."

Brett's backyard had a swing chair. It had a lot of cool stuff. Like a shiny metal table set, couches with overstuffed pillows, and even a fancy fireplace with blue flames. But my favorite was the swing chair. I liked the way it rocked back and forth when Brett pushed his feet off the ground.

It had stopped raining, and we wandered outside after his parents left, announcing they were going out for dinner. Now we were sitting on this chair while the sun set in front of us. That was another one of my favorite parts of his backyard: the view. There were no houses or buildings to see, just this far stretch of land that eventually turned into trees. It made the sunset look even more spectacular.

Usually, sunsets were gradual. Slowly the sky turned yellow, then pink, then orange before it all became black. Not tonight. Tonight, the sun set like someone hit the fast-forward button. The sky was blue one second, then blinding orange the next.

I don't know why I was so obsessed with the sky. Maybe it was the idea of a new day, a fresh start. Or maybe I just liked the way it looked. Not everything had to have some big meaning behind it.

When the sky was black, Brett said, "My dad's going to start staying here again." Then he pulled me closer until my back was to his chest. He was wearing a gray hoodie that smelled just like him. "And I got my essay back from Miss C. Got a B plus, thanks to you."

"It wasn't *all* me," I said.

I thought about telling Brett what I did today, visiting my dad, before deciding not to. For some reason, I wanted to keep that little piece to myself.

It started to rain again. I stood up, ready to head back inside, when Brett pulled me onto his lap. He was shaking his head, this evil smile on his face before he leaned in and kissed me. Even under the small cover of the swing, the wind blew the rain onto us. I could feel it on my neck, feel how wet Brett's hair was when I ran my fingers through it. I pressed my hand onto his heart and felt it beating right there, so close. I felt the way his fingers danced across the bare strip of skin above the waistband of my jeans.

I could feel everything.

I let my head fall back, felt the rain on my face for the second time that day. When I looked at Brett, there were droplets dripping down his face. His hair was flopping over his forehead and his eyes looked navy blue in the darkness. He was all skin and soft angles.

For some reason, my mind went back to that very first day, when I was sitting under the oak tree behind the football field. "I used to categorize my days," I told him. "Some were worth remembering and some I wanted to forget."

"Which one is today?" he asked.

I didn't even have to think about it. "One to remember."

Neither of us said anything for a moment. We sat there, staring at each other. There was beauty in the way his eyes held mine, in the way we held each other. Even when we didn't speak, it was still beautiful.

"Becca?" My name felt so familiar on his lips.

I nodded, wiping the hair off his forehead.

"I think I'm in love with you," he whispered, closing his eyes.

My heart seemed to leap out of my chest then. I was sure that if I looked up, I'd see it sailing past the stars, the moon. And when he kissed me, I searched for metaphors, for similes. For the "like" and the "as," but I couldn't think of a single thing but how it felt to have him so close to me. I searched for the words to put this feeling into thoughts and I came up empty. Or maybe I was just too full, full of whatever this feeling was.

Stop overthinking, I told myself. *Feel*.

So I did.

"I love you too," I said.

Brett smiled. The stars fell from the sky and landed on his face. It was the brightest smile of them all.

"You do?" he asked.

"I do," I said, laughing. "I don't think I even realized it until just now. But I do love you, Brett, because you make me feel safe. You make me feel *hopeful*. I never thought I'd love anyone. And with all the downsides of love, you managed to show me the upside," I whispered, holding his cheek in my palm, his heart in my hand.

Brett was watching me as if I were the sun his world revolved around, and I couldn't quite fathom how I'd ended up here. How, on a planet with billions of people whose lives would never cross, I managed to capture the heart of the most beautiful one.

I tilted my chin up as Brett leaned down, our lips yearning for each other's. His mouth met mine and my world exploded into a million tiny fragments. He tasted like peppermint, like home and every good thing mixed into one.

I wasn't sure how we ended up back inside his house or how the two of us fumbled up the stairs without falling and then tumbled onto his bed. His body felt so new, so right, and I let my hands trail across his skin like he was a map, undiscovered territory. When Brett lifted my shirt above my head, I felt myself blush, all the way from my cheeks to the tips of my toes.

"I don't want you to be embarrassed," he said, lifting his head from my chest until his eyes met mine. They were so dark, those black holes again. "I love every single thing about you."

I trembled as he kissed my jaw, my neck. I felt my armor cracking, every wall I'd built up around my heart tumbling down. His lips were undoing them, one by one, unraveling me from the inside out. And then his mouth crashed into mine and my entire world shattered. When the fragments blew away it was only Brett left, shining above me.

Brett

I REALIZED THAT NIGHT THERE was only one thing Becca needed to be happy. It wasn't me. It wasn't even books. It was the shocking, slightly disturbing obsession she had with cotton candy ice cream.

After she had showered and was drowning in my clothing, she sat down on the couch and hit me with those eyes, asking, "Brett, do you have any cotton candy ice cream?"

"We only provide quality ice cream in this household. But . . . I may have something even better. Wait here."

I ran up the stairs two at a time. I went to my bedroom and searched through my closet until I found it, tucked in the corner of the top shelf. It was the only book I would read as a kid. My mom was always buying me books to make up for all the hours I spent throwing a football around the backyard with my father. It didn't work. I always chose the football.

Book in hand, I raced back down the stairs and jumped over the back of the couch, landing beside Becca, who flinched. She was shaking her head—disapproving as always—as I placed the book in her lap. She picked it up quickly, running her fingers along the cover.

"'Goosebumps'?" she read aloud. I nodded proudly. "Why are you giving me this?" She tucked her foot under her thigh and turned to me.

"First of all," I said, "easy on the judgment, Hart. You're holding my childhood in your hands."

She giggled. Actually *giggled*. She even held the book up to cover her face.

"This is what you read as a kid?" she asked.

"That, and only that."

"Is this supposed to impress me?" she teased.

Yes. Was it working? "Have you read this?" I asked. She shook her head and I jerked my chin back toward my neck, disgusted. "Come on. Get comfy." I stretched into the corner of the couch, then patted my chest.

"What?"

"Get comfy," I repeated. "I'm reading this to you."

"I don't want to read that, Brett."

"Why? Because there's no romance? No *love*?" I said, wiggling my fingers. "I'm reading it *to* you, so there's nothing to complain about. All you need to do is listen to my voice."

Becca rolled her eyes. I was sure one day they'd get stuck like that.

"You really want to read to me?"

"No," I answered. "Believe me, there are a million things I'd rather do with you than read this book, but we kind of just did that, so . . . come here. You always tell me about your books; now give one of mine a try."

I was halfway through the second sentence when she said, "Wait. Is this scary?"

"These books are for children. And I thought you were all horror-movies-don't-scare-me tough?" I asked, raising my eyebrows.

"I am," she said, jabbing her elbow backward into my chest. It actually kind of hurt. "But words are scarier than images."

"I think you're the only person on this planet who thinks that."

"Look, an image is there in front of you. Right? You stare at it but then you can look away and it's gone," she said. "Words aren't like that. They build an entire world *around* you. It's not something you look at, it's something you're inside. That makes it scarier."

"I understood none of that."

She sighed. "Is it scary or not?"

"No, Becca. And if it is, I will protect you from all the fictional horror. Can I continue?"

"You seem very excited to read this."

She was right. I was. I loved the thought of sharing something that was important to me with her.

I rested one arm on the couch and wrapped the other one around her waist until she was caged against me, the book held in front of the two of us. When she nestled herself back into my chest, I continued reading. I was glad she didn't comment on how my voice sounded a little breathless. It was kind of pathetic what being so close to her did to me.

When I was halfway through the fifth chapter, Becca let out a long breath. It blew her hair around her face and it was like she finally let herself relax, let herself breathe. Her head rolled slightly to the side until her nose was pressed against my neck. I could feel her lips brush against my skin, feel her breath there too. Her hand slid up my chest and stopped over my heart. Then she just left it there.

I kept reading the entire time.

"Brett?"

"Yeah?"

"You've read the same sentence three times."

I had?

"Sorry," I mumbled. Her breath was still there, fanning across my neck. "You make it hard to concentrate."

"Do I?" she asked, lifting her head from my chest, pointing her chin up until her eyes met mine. They were darker than normal, like the sky after a rainstorm and the ocean, swirled into one. I could drown in them, I realized. I *was* drowning in them.

I really did love her. And here, in the darkness, it was like those words were all that existed. That and my heart beating too quickly. And Becca's lips too close. And the way her eyes fluttered closed for a second longer than normal after drifting to my mouth.

"Becca?"

"Yes?"

"No more pretending," I said. "No more faking. No more any of that."

Her eyebrows drew together. I ran my thumb across the lines. "I know that," she said, pausing to yawn. "Why are you saying this again?"

"Because I need you to know that this is real."

Then I kissed her, and it felt like I was sliding off the edge of the world.

Her eyes drooped closed, fingers slowly touching my cheeks, holding me to her. When I tugged her with me back onto the couch, until we were lying chest to chest, she let me, her mouth never leaving mine.

I could feel her hand slide from my face to my arm and stop there, holding me. *Good*, I thought, *don't let go*.

"It feels like the world is going to explode when I kiss you," I whispered.

"Then let it explode," she said.

I tugged her face back to mine and did just that.

Becca

I WAS SITTING UNDER THE oak tree behind the football field, watching practice. Tomorrow night was Brett's
first game back on the team. It was somewhat of a big deal.
His parents were going to be there. My mom and Cassie
were coming too. And it was weird, not being nervous for
our worlds to clash a little more. Slowly, I stopped trying to
keep my mom and Brett apart with a ten-foot pole.

They're both big parts of my life. A little crossover
couldn't hurt.

The team had been practicing for a while now—I'd
stopped paying attention after the first hour. Now I was
reading my book, whisked away into another world. I was

halfway through a page when I looked up to find Brett jogging toward me. The sun was making his hair shine that familiar golden hue.

"Shouldn't you be ripping your shirt off and running laps?" I called.

He was grinning, looming in front of me and hogging all the sun. "You'd like that, huh? Scoot over, let's share." I inched to my left, making room on the tree trunk for Brett to rest on. He was leaning back, eyes closed, out of breath.

"They're staring at you," I whispered, watching his teammates.

"Ignore them," he said, pressing his face into my neck. "Read to me."

"Shouldn't you keep practicing?"

"I've done enough drills for the day." He plucked the book from my hands, inspected the cover. "I recognize this one. Haven't you read this, like, a hundred times?"

"Twenty, actually," I said, snatching it back. "Today marks the twenty-first time."

He grinned. Shook his head.

"What?" I asked.

"Nothing. Nothing at all," he said, jerking his chin toward the book on my legs. "Read to me."

"Why?"

"Because you go somewhere else when you read. I want to go there with you."

We sat there and I read aloud, my back to Brett's chest. He pulled me a little closer, held me a little tighter. And this time, we escaped together.

Acknowledgments

Let's start at the beginning:

To Wattpad and Episode Interactive, the writing communities that allowed me to find my voice and a passion for words.

To the readers who stumbled across this book when it was nothing more than a rough draft published online with a different title. This book is ours, and I hope you approve, many drafts later!

To the incredible team at Wattpad that worked to turn a girl's pipe dream into reality. And Alysha, who was with me every step of the way.

To Catherine, my editor at HarperCollins, who took a very rough draft and sprinkled a little magic on it.

To my friends, you know who you are. The people that stayed up late with me brainstorming title ideas. Who offered endless pep talks and helped me write these very words. I couldn't have done it without you.

To Bella, Misty, and Chico, the greatest and furriest writing companions.

To my mom, who used to take me to the library every single week. And to the rest of my family, who didn't know about this book until the last minute. Sorry about that. Hey, did I mention I wrote a book?